D1606123

# Take the Bride

# Also from Carly Phillips

**The Knight Brothers**
Take Me Again
Take the Bride
Take Me Down
Dare Me Tonight

**Rosewood Bay**
Fearless
Breathe
Freed
Dream

**Bodyguard Bad Boys**
Rock Me
Tempt Me
His to Protect

**Dare to Love Series**
Dare to Love
Dare to Desire
Dare to Touch
Dare to Hold
Dare to Rock
Dare to Take

**Dare NY Series** (NY Dare Cousins)
Dare to Surrender
Dare to Submit
Dare to Seduce

**Billionaire Bad Boys**
Going Down Easy
Going Down Hard

Going Down Fast
Going In Deep

**Hot Zone Series**
Hot Stuff
Hot Number
Hot Item
Hot Property

**Lucky Series**
Lucky Charm
Lucky Streak
Lucky Break

# Take the Bride

## A Knight Brothers Novella

# By Carly Phillips

1001 Dark Nights

EVIL EYE
CONCEPTS

Take the Bride
A Knight Brothers Novella
By Carly Phillips

1001 Dark Nights
Copyright 2019 Carly Phillips
ISBN: 978-1-948050-94-4

Foreword: Copyright 2014 M. J. Rose
Published by Evil Eye Concepts, Incorporated

# Acknowledgments from the Author

Thank you Liz Berry and MJ Rose for making a dream come true. I'm thrilled to be part of the 1,001 Dark Nights family. It's truly an honor to be among such amazing talent and company. I'm so grateful!

Sign up for the 1001 Dark Nights Newsletter
and be entered to win a Tiffany Key necklace.

There's a contest every month!

Go to www.1001DarkNights.com to subscribe.

As a bonus, all subscribers can download
FIVE FREE exclusive books!

# One Thousand and One Dark Nights

*Once upon a time, in the future…*

*I was a student fascinated with stories and learning.
I studied philosophy, poetry, history, the occult, and
the art and science of love and magic. I had a vast
library at my father's home and collected thousands
of volumes of fantastic tales.*

*I learned all about ancient races and bygone
times. About myths and legends and dreams of all
people through the millennium. And the more I read
the stronger my imagination grew until I discovered
that I was able to travel into the stories… to actually
become part of them.*

*I wish I could say that I listened to my teacher
and respected my gift, as I ought to have. If I had, I
would not be telling you this tale now.
But I was foolhardy and confused, showing off
with bravery.*

*One afternoon, curious about the myth of the
Arabian Nights, I traveled back to ancient Persia to
see for myself if it was true that every day Shahryar
(Persian: شهریار, "king") married a new virgin, and then
sent yesterday's wife to be beheaded. It was written
and I had read, that by the time he met Scheherazade,
the vizier's daughter, he'd killed one thousand
women.*

*Something went wrong with my efforts. I arrived in the midst of the story and somehow exchanged places with Scheherazade – a phenomena that had never occurred before and that still to this day, I cannot explain.*

*Now I am trapped in that ancient past. I have taken on Scheherazade's life and the only way I can protect myself and stay alive is to do what she did to protect herself and stay alive.*

*Every night the King calls for me and listens as I spin tales. And when the evening ends and dawn breaks, I stop at a point that leaves him breathless and yearning for more. And so the King spares my life for one more day, so that he might hear the rest of my dark tale.*

*As soon as I finish a story... I begin a new one... like the one that you, dear reader, have before you now.*

# Chapter One

A cellist played Vivaldi's "The Four Seasons" as Sierra Knight's bridesmaids, her maid of honor, and the flower girl made their way down the aisle in a large church located in the Upper East Side of Manhattan.

Sierra couldn't see the procession but she'd been at the rehearsal, and she knew what was happening in the sanctuary of the church. From behind closed doors, where she stood with her oldest brother, Ethan, the deep strains of the string instrument reverberated around her, her heart beating hard and fast in her chest.

She smoothed a hand down her fit-and-flair style wedding gown with lace and beading that she'd loved the moment she'd slid it on. The cathedral-length veil in tulle was matched by the long train flowing behind her. She'd never felt more beautiful... or more nervous.

"Are you sure this is what you want?" Ethan asked, obviously reading her nerves as he put a hand on her trembling arm. "The car's out front, the engine's running," he said, half joking, but she heard the serious note in his voice.

As her oldest brother, he was the father figure she'd always needed since their own parent never lived up to the role. Although Alexander Knight was sitting in one of the pews up front with wife number four, he wasn't the man Sierra wanted walking her down the aisle. He hadn't earned that honor nor had he seemed insulted that he hadn't been asked to play the traditional role.

She thought about Ethan's question, swallowed hard, and nodded. "Jason is a great guy," she said, meaning every word.

She'd been with Jason Armstrong, a lawyer, for over a year and she knew him well. They'd met through friends and begun dating soon after. He had a calming presence and he catered to her every desire. He was a kind, decent man.

"I know I'll have a good life with him," she reassured her brother, glancing at his strong jaw, which he'd set as he narrowed his gaze.

"I married a woman I thought I knew," Ethan said, digging into his own pain to make sure Sierra was okay. "Mandy wasn't who I believed she was. I just want you to be sure you want to marry him."

Ethan had recently lost his wife to an accidental drug overdose, then gone on to find out she'd been having an affair and stealing from the family company to subsidize her drug addiction. He was not only grieving, he was coming to terms with the betrayal.

But his words now were coming from an honest and good place, one of love. "Don't get me wrong," he continued. "I like Jason. We all do," he said, referring to her two other brothers, Parker and Sebastian. "But are you passionately in love with him?"

She did her best not to blush at the question asked by her brother. He pushed the point, forcing Sierra to wonder if Ethan saw something in her relationship she hadn't wanted to acknowledge.

But she shook her head, ignoring the sudden burning behind her eyes. "Not everyone gets passion, Ethan. It's fine," she said softly. "I'll be fine." So why did she have a case of anxiety? Why was her chest weighty and heavy?

The music transitioned from Vivaldi to the more traditional "Here Comes the Bride," and Sierra drew a steadying breath.

It was time.

The heavy wooden doors were opened, and beyond her veil,

she faced the room full of family and friends who stood as one, the sounds of them shifting positions echoing in the large room.

With Ethan by her side, she began the long walk down the aisle, taking her time as she'd been instructed at rehearsal. She looked at the familiar faces around her, some of whom she worked with at Knight Time Technology, where she was head of the Social Media Division, some who were extended family, others friends from high school and college.

As she approached the front rows, her gaze landed on the one man she shouldn't think about today.

Ryder Hammond.

Her brother Sebastian's best friend.

Her high school boyfriend.

Her first love.

She swallowed over the sudden lump in her throat, unable not to compare his rugged good looks to the man waiting for her at the end of the aisle. Jason, lean and handsome in his tuxedo, his blond hair neatly trimmed, his face perfectly shaved, his gaze patiently on hers.

Then there was Ryder. His jet-black hair was too long to be considered neat, but it suited his sexy features, as did the stubble he hadn't shaved on his face. His suit jacket fit him perfectly, accentuating muscles he'd achieved by working in construction when, at this point in his career, he could sit behind a desk if he chose. He liked to build with his hands. Hands she was intimately familiar with, and at the thought, her nipples tightened beneath her dress.

His green eyes locked on hers, a wave of what looked like longing flashing in his gaze. She could once read every emotion on his face, but she didn't know now whether it was her mind conjuring what she wanted to see or whether desire was, in fact, what he was thinking and feeling now. They both knew that a big wedding had once been their dream. Or at least it had been the fantasy she'd woven for them both and he'd let her.

A small tremor rippled through her at the thought, the

memory of them lying under the big tree in her backyard as she detailed her idea of a perfect day. Sierra and Ryder, she'd thought, had been meant to be. Until he'd broken up with her and ripped her heart to shreds at the same time.

Ethan paused at the slight shudder that overtook her. "Are you sure?" he whispered, so low only she could hear.

"I have to be," she replied just as softly.

With a half shake of his head, he continued their path to Jason. The man she was marrying.

Another few steps and Ethan paused at the end of the aisle, lifted her veil, and kissed her cheek. "Be happy," he whispered. "I love you."

And then he handed her off to her groom.

She met Jason's gaze and took his hand, smiling, her nerves settling down as they took their places. He was solid and secure, everything she needed and wanted in her life. Her father had given her a revolving door of so-called mother figures who wanted nothing to do with her as she grew up. He hadn't had any more time for her than they had. And so she'd dreamed of marrying one man and living the happily ever after that had eluded her father after her mom passed away.

She pushed useless thoughts of the past aside. She had no reason to question her decision to marry Jason, who offered her exactly what she craved. It had just been last-minute jitters that had hit her before, Ryder merely a reminder of adolescent daydreams.

Her thoughts were normal for any bride, she thought, as the priest began to speak. Jason held her hand and she looked into his eyes, the ceremony going on as planned, as the words were spoken around them.

"If anyone can show just cause why this couple cannot lawfully be joined together in matrimony, let them speak now or forever hold their peace."

Sierra's gaze shot to the priest in annoyance. She'd specifically asked for that line to be omitted, along with anything else that was sexist, such as her obeying her groom.

She blew out a harsh breath, realizing the priest was still waiting, glancing around the room.

It was as if an invisible pull had her looking away from Jason, turning, her gaze locking with Ryder's.

What happened next occurred in slow motion.

"I do," Ryder said, rising to his feet.

He did not just say that, she thought, panic setting in, her stare still joined with his.

"What the hell?" Jason asked, sounding pissed off.

"Sir?" the priest asked, clearly taken off guard. After all, how many times did an actual objection occur except on TV?

"I object," Ryder said, loud and clear.

People pointed and whispered.

"Fuck," Sebastian said from his place beside her brothers and Matthew, Jason's best man.

Suddenly chaos erupted around them. Ryder started forward at the same time Jason lunged toward him. His best man grabbed him, holding him back from going after Ryder, whose sister, Skye, one of Sierra's bridesmaids, ran for her brother.

"Calm down," she heard Matthew say.

Sebastian, she noted, went directly for Ryder, stopping him from getting near her as he spoke to him. Sebastian's wife, Ashley, came up beside him.

"Honey, are you okay?" Maggie, her bridesmaid and wedding planner, grasped her hand.

She turned to her friend, who looked beautiful in the deep purple dress Sierra had chosen. "I don't know," she said. And she didn't.

What had Ryder been thinking, objecting at her wedding?

"Oh, shit. Lena's diving into the flowers!" Rayna, her maid of honor and best friend since high school, cried, causing Maggie to leave Sierra's side and help their friend run for the little girl, who, unattended, was pulling petals from the floral arrangements.

"Someone call an ambulance! Candy's feeling faint!" Sierra's father's voice boomed through the church.

A glance told Sierra that her stepmother, an attention-seeking whore who'd worn white to the wedding, something Sierra knew because they'd stopped by the bridal room to see her, was fanning herself and causing her own scene.

"Go," Sierra said to Joy, her final bridesmaid, who was standing around wringing her hands. "Call 911 for my dad."

Sierra looked to Ryder again, who was deep in conversation with Sebastian, Parker, and Ethan, who, if Ryder was lucky, wouldn't beat him to a pulp for humiliating her this way. Suddenly he glanced up and met her gaze, those green eyes looking into her soul. He'd once known her better than anyone.

She'd even dreamed of walking down the aisle to him, and her stomach twisted with an unexpected pang of regret. She stared into his handsome face, his eyes never leaving hers, and a shock of longing slid through her.

Shaken, she tore her gaze from his and headed directly for Jason, stopping in front of him.

His face was red from anger, his best man still had a hand on his shoulder, and his sister was standing beside him.

"What's going on?" Ethan came to her side and faced Jason, wrapping an arm around Sierra.

"Jason, we can continue where we left off," she said, meeting his gaze.

His face contorted with hurt. "Seriously? Do you think I didn't notice you looking at him when you were walking down the aisle to me?" he yelled, outraged, startling Sierra with his outburst.

"Wait, what?" He was angry with her?

Her brother's supportive hold on her tightened.

"The priest asked if anyone objected, and you turned around and fucking looked at him." She'd never seen Jason this furious.

But, oh God, she had turned and looked at Ryder. But she hadn't wanted to end the ceremony. Yes, she'd thought about Ryder briefly as she'd walked down the aisle. She'd had a moment when she remembered the past, but she'd headed toward her future. Toward him.

Ryder showed up just then, facing Jason.

"It's him." Jason pointed, shoving his finger into Ryder's chest. "It's always been fucking him. At every family function, always around. You wanted him to interrupt the wedding," he said, accusing her of being at fault.

Ryder appeared about to grab Jason's finger when Sebastian pulled him back. "Don't," her brother muttered.

Sierra blinked, tears in her eyes. This couldn't be happening. Her life was falling apart and she had no way to stop it.

\* \* \* \*

*Oh, shit. What the fuck did I just do?*

Ryder Hammond stared into the eyes of his best friend, who appeared ready to murder him. Next to Sebastian were his two brothers, looking equally furious, and Ryder knew he was in deep shit.

Had he really just objected at Sierra's wedding?

He began to sweat beneath his suit. But he'd done it, the words had spilled forth, and now he had to dissect why. Ignoring the swearing men beside him, Ryder thought about the moment the big wooden double doors had opened and he'd seen Sierra in her wedding gown.

Her long light brown hair tumbled over her shoulders in perfect curls, her curves showing in her fitted dress, her cleavage just appropriately peeking out from the dipped neckline. Her gorgeous face had glowed as she walked down the aisle to another man.

He'd come today because, as a close family friend, he'd been invited. Because he thought he'd made his peace with the way things had ended between them. And for closure. Once she was married, she'd be lost to him forever. And that was the thought that had run through his head at the moment the priest asked if anyone objected.

He hadn't planned to open his mouth.

He hadn't meant to ruin her wedding.

He had intended to watch her be given away to another man and, dammit, be okay with it.

But he wasn't.

So here they were.

He glanced at her brothers, Sebastian, his closest friend, and Parker, because Ethan had gone after his sister. "I have to talk to her."

"No fucking way," Sebastian said, one palm on his chest, blocking him from moving forward.

"If I knew you'd planned this shit, I never would have let you in the door," said Parker.

Ryder held up both hands. "It wasn't planned. The words just came out of my mouth. But now that I said them, I need to speak with your sister." He shoved past the brothers and headed directly for Sierra, who stood talking to the man she was supposed to marry.

His gaze locked with hers but Jason wasn't having it.

"It's him." He pointed, shoving his finger into Ryder's chest. "It's always been fucking him. At every family function, always around." Jason turned to Sierra. "You wanted him to interrupt the wedding." He was clearly furious.

Ryder would be fucking livid if the situation had been reversed, and he had a moment's pity for the man, already opting not to grab his finger and break it when Sebastian pulled him back.

He didn't need Sebastian's muttered word, "Don't," to tell him to behave.

"I'm out of here," Jason, the groom, muttered.

"What?" Sierra cried, stricken, and the sound went straight to Ryder's gut.

"You don't want to marry me or this whole mess would have ended up differently," Jason said, turning and storming out, his best man and sister rushing after him.

Tears streamed down Sierra's face as she glared at Ryder. "How could you?"

"Come on," Sebastian said, his hand on Ryder's shoulder. "Let's go somewhere and talk."

Ryder shook his head, determined to talk to Sierra.

"Don't do this unless your intentions are fucking good," Sebastian muttered.

Ryder glanced at Sierra, who looked distraught and upset, causing his stomach to churn with the knowledge that he'd caused her pain. That had never been his intent, if he'd had any intention at all.

But he shook his head. He wasn't finished here. "I need to talk to you," he said, glancing only at her.

"You don't have to say anything to him." Ethan had his arm around her, holding her upright.

Her eyes were narrowed, her lips pursed. He remembered that look, one that would often end up with them in a heated kiss or resulting in hot and heavy angry sex. She was pissed as hell. But she wasn't storming away.

He extended his hand toward her, needing the moment alone.

Sierra stared at him and he looked back, their gazes locked in a way only they could understand.

"Five minutes," she muttered.

Glaring, she ignored his outstretched hand and stormed past him, her gown with the long train trailing behind her as she headed for the dressing room.

Despite her anger, she was willing to talk, which told him one thing.

There was still something between them.

Something, he could work with, he thought, and followed her out.

The moment he joined her in the small room, Sierra spun to glare at him. "How could you do this to me?" she asked, face flushed, eyes wide and glassy, makeup stains on her cheeks. She was beautiful despite her tears.

He shoved his hands into his front pants pockets. Meeting her gaze, he opted for the truth. "It wasn't planned."

"Oh, that makes it better," she muttered. "You ruined my wedding on a whim."

He ran a hand over his face, knowing that despite the blurted-out objection, the feelings behind it were real. "The priest's words were a wakeup call," he said.

She blinked at his comment. "For who?" she asked. "You made your choice years ago and it wasn't me."

He winced at the reminder of all he'd thrown away, no matter that he'd made the decision for all the right reasons. But he didn't have time to dwell on the past now.

She turned to head back inside the church and panic struck him. He knew if she walked away, it would be for the last time.

"Sierra, wait."

She glanced over her shoulder and he knew he had mere seconds to convince her not to leave.

"Do you really want to go back into that room with all the chaos and insanity waiting for you?" he asked. "Your stepmother is splayed out on the floor, moaning and waiting for paramedics to tell her she's fine. The flower girl is having a meltdown. Your brothers are plotting to kill me, and you have a room full of people in there who expected a wedding."

She shuddered at the reminders. "Then I want to go home."

He raised an eyebrow. "Where your bags are packed and your things are in boxes so you can move in with the same groom who just abandoned you instead of fighting for you?"

Tears filled her eyes as she met his gaze. "I hate you."

His chest squeezed at her blurted-out words. "No, you don't, but I understand why you want to think you do."

She glared at him. "So what are you suggesting?"

"Let me get you out of here. Give everyone a chance to calm down and think. Let cooler heads prevail."

She glanced toward the sanctuary, where the sounds of chaos still carried to them.

"Come on." He held out a hand, and this time she placed her palm in his, the warmth and electrical connection between them instantaneous despite the wary expression on her face and the emotional walls between them.

Before her brothers could burst into the room, he led her outside and toward his car, helping her climb in and tucking her dress inside before shutting the door.

He had her where he wanted her. He just didn't know what he was going to do next.

\* \* \* \*

With no destination in mind, Ryder drove them over the George Washington Bridge and out of New York City. Beside him, Sierra sat, her dress fluffed around her, staring out the window, not saying a word.

Except to hand her his phone and tell her to text her brothers and let them know she was okay, he left her alone, hoping she wasn't stewing and building up a case of righteous anger against him. He wanted the chance later for them to really talk.

He was surprised when, after about half an hour, she fell asleep, leaving him to his own thoughts and self-recriminations, and he had many, not all revolving around his actions at the wedding.

He glanced over, taking in her delicate profile, noticing the freckles on her nose, remembering how he'd pretend to count them, one by one. He swallowed a groan, not wanting to wake her up, but asking himself, how the hell had they gotten to this point?

He gripped the wheel tighter, the past coming back to him. As Sebastian's best friend, he'd been around the Knight house all the time when they were growing up. Two years apart, he couldn't help but notice as Sierra matured into a gorgeous woman. He'd been attracted to her and knew better than to screw around when it came to his best friend's sister, but when they finally did get together, it was in a relationship.

And her brothers, knowing him as they did, had actually approved of them as a couple. They'd trusted Ryder to do right by her. Crazily enough, knowing that had played into the decisions he'd made.

Although his family wasn't as wealthy as Sebastian's, his dad had done well until a market crash hit and his business took a dive. He should have gone away to school, but his dad had had a heart attack before he could leave and Ryder had stayed home to help run the family business with his older brother, Andrew. His father had developed a weak heart, resulting in many hospital trips over the years, and Ryder had never regretted his decision.

At his older sibling's urging, Ryder had gone to school at night, earning his undergraduate and master's degrees, but during the day, he'd worked overseeing the day-to-day construction side of the business while his brother handled the office management part of the company.

And during the summer before Sierra's senior year, they'd first gotten together. As the school year began, she'd applied to college, always planning to go to school away from home. Even before they'd been a couple, she'd talked about how eager she'd been to finally get away and have independence without three older brothers watching over her. But their romance had taken a turn neither had expected, getting hot and heavy quickly.

He'd fallen hard and fast for the girl with the beautiful face and the big heart. They'd both lost their moms at a young age, hers to cancer, his to a freak car accident, and they'd had that loss in common. Because her family had money, which included having a housekeeper and a cook, there was always food left over after dinner. And she'd insisted on bringing meals to his dad when he came home from one of his frequent hospital trips.

Before Ryder knew it, they'd found themselves making plans for the future. She'd detailed the wedding of her dreams and he hadn't freaked that she wanted to spend the rest of her life with him. He'd wanted the same thing. There'd been something deep and meaningful between them from the beginning that had only grown over time.

Except that Sierra had started to talk about staying home and attending a local college instead of going away and being exposed to all the things she'd wanted before they'd gotten together—college, independence, life, and yes, dammit, other guys. She needed to experience more before she committed to him. She needed to be certain of what she wanted, and as a senior in high school, she couldn't possibly know what was best for her.

Ryder never wanted her to resent him for holding her back, so he'd broken up with her so she could live her original dreams, crushing his own heart in the process.

Knowing he'd lost her for good, he'd gone on with his life, and though that had included being with other women, none had ever come close to making him feel what she had. Over the years, he'd watched her date other men, knowing he'd lost his chance, that she still harbored anger and resentment despite putting up with him for Sebastian's sake. When she'd ended up engaged, he'd known it really was over for them. No someday in their future. Until he'd opened his mouth at the wedding.

He glanced up, realizing he'd been driving for over an hour. He was on Route 80 in New Jersey, signs for the Delaware Water Gap and the Poconos ahead of him.

Shit.

He glanced over to the passenger side of the car. Sierra was still asleep. She was going to fucking kill him when she realized where they'd ended up, but what the hell.

He only had one chance to win her back, and he couldn't do it in the city with her surrounded by her brothers and friends. Instead he was headed another thirty minutes away to a mountain resort that he was pretty sure was the cheesiest honeymoon capital of the northeast. A place that advertised heart-shaped bathtubs and themed rooms.

A place where they could be alone.

# Chapter Two

Sierra woke up as the car turned off, the motor coming to a stop. She shook her head and looked around at the unfamiliar surroundings. Trees were visible outside the windows, and a glittering sign said *Paradise Cove*, and beneath it, *A Couples Only Poconos Resort.*

"You have got to be kidding me!" She glanced at Ryder in disbelief. "What the hell are we doing in the Poconos?" She'd obviously fallen asleep for a good two hours, the shock of the day along with the glass of champagne she'd had prior to the non-wedding catching up with her.

He treated her to his most charming grin. "You always said you wanted to honeymoon here. That it was romantic."

"I was seventeen!" she yelled at him. "I didn't know any better. And we aren't on our honeymoon." She glanced down at her white wedding gown, not missing the irony of the situation but in no mood to find it funny.

She and Jason were supposed to be on their way to St. Lucia tomorrow morning. Instead she was in the honeymoon capital of Pennsylvania. Her stomach cramped at the reminder of all she'd left behind earlier today. Although she'd texted Sebastian from Ryder's phone, she hoped her brothers weren't too worried about her. She'd left her own phone in the bridal room and couldn't know whether Jason had tried to reach her or not. But her brothers knew she was with Ryder, and if Jason wanted her, he certainly could contact them and find out how to talk to her.

Instead she was in the Poconos with her ex. She looked at the man who'd driven her over one hundred miles from home and waited for an explanation.

He placed an arm behind her seat, turning to face her. "By the time I realized how far I'd driven, we were half an hour from here. I couldn't think of anywhere else to crash. And I wasn't about to turn around and drive another two hours home."

She frowned at him. "So now what? You expect me to stay here with you?"

"Would it really be so bad?" he asked, his voice gentling. "I understand you're angry with me, but we're here. It's late. Let's just go inside and see if we can get a room."

The very idea of it was crazy. Nothing good could come of her being alone with Ryder now, and she really shouldn't have left with him. But it was too late to take her actions back now.

She blew out a resigned breath. "Fine. But I hope they have a gift shop," she muttered, needing a change of clothes because nothing about this trip had been thought through.

She climbed out of the car and Ryder helped her gather the train and fold it up so she could hold it over one arm. Then together, they walked into the main area of the resort and headed to the reception desk.

"I assume you have a reservation?" the woman behind the counter asked, her gaze traveling over Ryder in his suit, Sierra in her white gown.

"Umm, no. But we'd like a room for a couple of days," Ryder said with a smile.

"One night," Sierra countered.

He frowned at her and the girl behind the desk looked confused. She typed something into the computer and glanced up at them. "Our honeymoon suite is booked and we only have suites, not rooms, but I'm sure you'll love what's available. All of our suites have round king-size beds beneath celestial ceilings, log-burning fireplaces, and heart-shaped tubs or champagne-glass-shaped whirlpool spas."

Sierra felt her mouth drop open at the description. It was everything she'd seen in commercials as a young, love-struck girl dreaming of romance.

"I don't think—"

"We'll take one," he said, cutting her off.

The clerk looked back and forth between them, a definite furrow between her eyebrows. "We can only offer you two nights. I'm sorry but we're booked after that."

Before she could utter another word, Ryder slid his credit card across the counter. "We'll stay both nights. And the airline lost our luggage, so do you think you could hook us up with the basics?" he asked.

She was grateful he was thinking of everything, even if she was still annoyed with him. Besides, she was beyond uncomfortable in the wedding gown, and Sierra hoped the woman could help them.

The clerk's gaze softened at the mention of missing suitcases. "That's awful and frustrating. I'll send up toiletries and amenities," the woman said. "There are bathrobes in the rooms, and the gift shop and stores open tomorrow morning. You'll be able to pick up more things to wear then."

"Thank you," Sierra said, appreciating the woman's kindness.

"We're grateful for anything you can do," Ryder said.

He slipped a tip across the counter and the clerk glanced down and grinned at him. "Thank you. I'll call housekeeping right now. In the meantime, here are your key cards. Breakfast and dinner are included. A continental breakfast is served in the room tomorrow. I'll even throw in some parts of our honeymoon package," she whispered to Ryder, making Sierra wonder how much money he'd given her.

No matter the amount, she had no intention of making use of their specialty package, she thought, exhaustion seeping into her bones despite her long nap. The day had been overwhelming and was definitely catching up with her.

She unwittingly sagged against him, and his arm immediately came out, wrapping around her, holding her for the first time in forever. It took all her willpower not to lean her head against him and let him take over.

"Come on, sweetheart. You look dead on your feet," Ryder said, and taking her by surprise, he swept her into his arms.

Just like a real bride.

Although she wanted to argue, she was just beginning to realize how much her feet ached from the high-heeled designer shoes she'd worn. Keeping her mouth shut and letting him hold her had nothing to do with how much she liked the feel of his strong arms wrapped around her. Or the notion of being carried across the threshold of their romantic suite.

Once more, she pushed the thought of what should have been happening tonight aside. It didn't matter whether or not Jason would have carried her over the threshold or let her walk across on her own. He'd abandoned her, she thought, and to her surprise, tears stung her eyes.

Despite being prepared, when they walked inside, the over-the-top décor took her by surprise. The room was red and white, from the bedding on the circular mattress to the drapes hanging over the windows and the red lacquer dressers and night tables.

Across the room she saw the bathtub reachable by a set of stairs. "Oh my God."

"Welcome to the Champagne Tower Suite," Ryder said, lowering her carefully to her feet.

"That's obscene," she muttered.

"Or sexy," he whispered in her ear.

She trembled, nipples puckering, and she stepped aside, annoyed with her body's reaction to him. Feet cramping, she immediately kicked off her heels and pushed them to the corner of the room.

She didn't know how she was going to survive the romance of

this place with Ryder staying in the same room with her. Yes, it was cheesy, but there was something romantic about it if she let her imagination run away with her, and surrounded by the color of hearts and flowers, which sat on the table, it was hard not to. Especially since she used to fantasize about honeymooning here with him.

"Are you hungry?" he asked, drawing her attention.

She glanced over her shoulder. "I don't know if I'm more hungry or tired. I'm afraid I'll fall asleep before we even get room service delivered."

His gaze softened. "Let's just put in for an early breakfast."

"Sounds good." She glanced at the bed, realizing they were obviously going to be sharing that cozy mattress. She also knew she couldn't sleep in a heavy terrycloth robe, which meant she was climbing into that bed in her bra and panties. She blushed at the thought.

"Your cheeks are pink. What's going through your mind?" he asked.

She pulled her bottom lip between her teeth. "I have nothing to sleep in."

His gaze darkened. "You can wear my shirt."

She shook her head. She wasn't about to cuddle up and be surrounded by his masculine scent. It was going to be hard enough to sleep beside him.

"I can't sleep when I feel confined," she said, using a legitimate and acceptable excuse that wouldn't embarrass her. She normally got in bed wearing a short silk camisole that she barely felt on her skin. "I'll make do. Can you help me get out of this dress?"

He walked up behind her and she was immediately aware of him, the warmth of his body as he came close. "Lift your hair," he said in a gruff voice.

She raised the heavy strands and pulled them over her shoulder, then felt his big hands come to the tiny buttons that began midway down her back. He struggled with the size of them, muttering as he worked, his breath warm as he leaned closer for a better look.

His scent was familiar and arousing, her imagination running away as his hands touched the buttons the way they'd once danced over her skin. Her entire body felt like it was on fire, awareness sizzling through her veins. Need pulsing inside her. Her thong panties were damp, her nipples hard, desire a living, breathing thing inside her . . .

In all her time with Jason, she'd never experienced passion like she had with Ryder, and the fact that just his nearness had her hyperaware of him put her on alert to the fact that her feelings for him hadn't dissipated in the time they'd been apart.

"There. Finished."

Ryder stepped back and she nearly sagged with relief. She'd come so close to turning around and plastering herself against him, reliving a past that she'd never quite gotten over.

It had been one thing for her to acknowledge to her brother that she didn't share a passionate love with Jason, but to experience the difference now with Ryder was disconcerting. Just a few touches from Ryder made her truly realize exactly how much she'd been willing to give up in her marriage.

And on that thought... "I'm going to the bathroom and I'd like to climb into the bed without you watching."

He frowned. "I just unbuttoned your dress lower than your ass. Besides, what I haven't seen just now, I've seen before," he reminded her.

"Not lately you haven't." She stormed into the bathroom and slammed the door behind her, frustrated with herself for feeling anything for him at all.

Before she could even let the dress slide off her shoulders, a knock sounded on the bathroom door. "What?" she called out.

"Housekeeping brought some toiletries," he said.

"Thanks," she said, accepting the Paradise-Cove-labeled bag through the door and then shutting it quickly, luckily not catching his hand as she did.

A little while later, she'd brushed her teeth, washed her face, and cleaned up after the long day. After hanging her dress on the hook behind the door, she stepped back into the room to find he was already in bed. His bare chest peeked out from beneath the red satin comforter as he waited for her to join him, tanned and muscular and more appealing than she wanted him to be.

Those strong arms had once held her tight, given her comfort, and caused her arousal. She wished what she felt was only sexual, but this was the man she'd loved and had dreamed of spending the rest of her life with in a way much different than the plans she'd made with Jason.

After the breakup, she'd spent years seeing him with Sebastian, blocking out her feelings for him, and ignoring the pang of regret that inevitably came with him being near. She hadn't been the one to end things, and despite being hurt by his actions, her feelings hadn't turned off as easily as she'd wanted them to. Viewing him in that luxurious bed now was like a punch in the stomach, creating a yearning she'd tried to push away a long time ago.

"Shut your eyes," she bit out, knowing she was being childish, but she didn't care. She wasn't ready to parade in front of him in the see-through bra and panties she'd bought to wear beneath her wedding gown, for her wedding night. With another man.

She shuddered at the thought, wondering why she hadn't spent more time mourning Jason's loss than she had thinking about being in a honeymoon suite with her first love. Ryder had ruined her wedding and the future she'd had planned... and yet she'd left the church with him willingly. She didn't like herself very much right now.

"Come on," Ryder said, placing his hand over his eyes. "They're closed." He'd shut off the overhead lights in the room, leaving the lamp on by the nightstand.

Having no choice but to trust him not to peek, she walked out and came to the bed, sliding into the satin sheets. She pulled the comforter up around her and sighed. "I'm good."

He lowered his arm and met her gaze, his expression contrite.

"It's going to be okay," he said, although he couldn't know any such thing.

"So now you can read the future?"

"I wish," he muttered. "No. I just have faith. For now, though, can we just get some sleep?"

"Yeah." She knew they'd have plenty of time to talk tomorrow, although she wasn't looking forward to a rehash of the past or the present. But maybe for both of their sakes, they needed to resolve their issues and her anger over the end of the relationship once and for all. So that she could figure out what she really wanted for her future, though she was beginning to suspect that it wasn't with Jason, a man who'd so easily walked away from her at the first sign of trouble.

Turning on her side away from him, she punched the pillows and curled into the soft sheets. She was exhausted from the events of the day, which should be running through her head. The loss of the future she'd planned, the things at home waiting for her, presents to return, apologies to be made, boxes to unpack. But those things weren't first and foremost on her mind.

Because when she breathed in deep, she smelled the musky scent of the man beside her. And whether it was her imagination or not, she imagined she could feel the warmth of him beside her. Her body was well aware of his presence, and her heart banged loudly in her chest, anxiety clawing at her, not because of what she'd lost but because of the possible reasons Ryder had objected at her wedding.

Like it or not, he was back in her life. She didn't know what she'd be doing with him… and that was the real cause of the apprehension keeping her awake. Not the man shifting beside her, also unable to sleep.

\* \* \* \*

Ryder woke up to Sierra wrapped around him, her mostly naked body plastered to his, his cock hard, morning wood making itself known. It'd taken him forever to fall asleep last night. He was too aware of the woman curled away from him, trying her best to stick to her side of the bed. So he was shocked now that her head was in the crook of his arm, her hands on his chest, her knee hiked up over his legs.

When he heard a knock on the door, he assumed it was room service bringing breakfast. He slid out from beneath her, and though she shifted and moaned, winding herself around the pillow instead of him, she didn't wake up.

The waiter set up their continental breakfast on the table before accepting a tip and leaving him alone. He took in the double coffee cups, the muffins and croissants and other baked goods, and headed back to see if Sleeping Beauty was awake.

He stepped over to the bed and eased himself down onto the mattress. The round shape was disconcerting. He settled back against the pillows, and no sooner had he relaxed than Sierra rolled back, positioning herself against him once more. They hadn't slept in the same bed in the past. She'd been a senior in high school and her spending the night wasn't an option. But when they'd lie outside in her backyard, this was the position she'd take.

Wrapping an arm around her, he closed his eyes and breathed in her sweet scent, different now but no less alluring. She appealed to him on many levels beyond sexual. Her sharp mind, her normally sweet personality, although he understood why she wasn't treating him to that part of her now. She loved family the way he did, wanted similar things out of their future. He knew because she'd laid it all out for him once upon a time.

And he'd thrown it all away. For good reasons, but it didn't make him feel any better or change their situation now.

He must have fallen back to sleep, and when he woke up, they were wound around each other still.

Sierra's eyes opened wide and she attempted to pull away but he held on tight. "Don't."

With a resigned sigh, she laid her head against his chest. "What are we doing?" she asked him, voice calmer than yesterday.

She was obviously more relaxed and accepting of their situation than she'd been.

"We are exploring our options. Seeing what's still between us."

"We are?"

"You tell me." He was putting out feelers, testing where she was when it came to him.

She swallowed hard, her throat moving against his skin. "I don't know, Ryder. You can't just interrupt my wedding and now say we're going to see what's still between us."

At her unwillingness to fall in line with the plans he wanted, his heart kicked harder in his chest. "Tell me something."

"Hmm?"

"I know I ruined your big day." There was no getting past that. "But did I… I mean, were you really in love with him?"

It was a stupid question. On the one hand, she'd been in a wedding dress, ready to commit her life to the other man. On the other, she had gotten into the car with him, so Ryder held his breath for her answer.

"I was going to marry Jason."

She pushed herself up and away from him, and he didn't pull her back.

Yet.

"Yes, but what was between you? Were you in love?" he asked again, needing answers. He couldn't keep her here just because he needed to see if there was a second chance for them. Not if she'd truly been in love with someone else.

She blew out a long breath. "Right before the doors opened, Ethan asked me if I was sure." Not meeting his gaze, she said, "It gave me pause and I… I had second thoughts."

She lifted her face to him and tears shimmered in her pretty blue eyes. "It's not that I didn't love Jason. We were compatible. He offered me everything I wanted in my life."

"Security and a future aren't enough to base a lifetime on." He named the minimal things she would want in order to marry someone because he knew her that well. He had. He still did.

She sniffed. "Yes, well, it seemed enough at the time. I do love him," she said, her words a knife to Ryder's chest.

"But you aren't in love with him."

"How do you know that?" she asked, some of the fire from last night back in her tone.

He rolled his shoulders. "Easy. Because when he walked out on you, you let him go." He debated his next words, then decided it wasn't the time to hold anything back. "When I broke up with you, you didn't let me go as easily." He shuddered at the memories of a time that had nearly killed him. "But you stood in a wedding dress and you let Jason walk out the door."

She blinked and the tears she'd been holding back rolled down her cheeks. He swept one away with his finger.

"I was in shock."

"Maybe. You also got in the car with me. Was that because you were in shock?"

She glared at him but it didn't last long.

He didn't want to push her further. He already had his answer about her second thoughts.

It was all he needed for now.

\* \* \* \*

Before Sierra could reply to Ryder's comment, her stomach grumbled loudly and she groaned at the sound. "I'm starving."

His lips curved in a smile. "Well, it's a good thing breakfast is already here." After swinging his legs over the side of the mattress, he walked to the table and returned with a tray full of food, placing it down on the bed.

She pulled her gaze away from his tight ass in his boxer briefs, clenching her teeth at the intimacy he was clearly already comfortable with. She wasn't. Instead she pulled the covers up higher, covering her breasts and her bra.

"I can't promise the coffee is still hot, but there's enough pastries and muffins in here to quiet the beast," he said with a laugh.

She glared at his joke about her noisy stomach, then turned to focus on the food he placed on the bed before climbing back into his side.

Picking which kind of muffin she wanted was a welcome, easy decision. Because as she ate—a blueberry muffin and then a scone, making up for not eating much at all yesterday—she was tortured by facts that were hard to admit to.

She'd rolled into Ryder in her sleep. She'd willingly turned to him in a way she'd never gone to Jason—they'd slept on separate sides of the bed, coming together to have sex when they were due, not out of some sense of innate need that couldn't be contained.

When she looked back on yesterday, walking down the aisle after Ethan had asked if Jason was the man she really wanted, she hadn't been sure. And when push came to shove, instead of fighting for her, Jason had stormed out, leaving her to Ryder. The guy who hadn't let her marry another man.

That told her where she stood with her groom now. Not that they didn't need to talk and have a rational conversation, if such a thing were possible. But she knew they were over. How could they be anything but? The truth hurt along with the loss of the future she'd clearly seen laid out for herself.

She glanced at Ryder as he watched her quietly. He'd always known when to talk and when to stay silent, reading her mind in ways Jason never had. She rubbed her eyes, wondering now why she'd thought settling emotionally or physically was enough for her. She ripped a piece of croissant off the end of the roll and shoved it into her mouth. No more carbs, she thought, finally feeling full.

She studied him through lowered lashes, knowing that they hadn't yet had the much-needed conversation about their past. Given that she wasn't ready to go home and face the ramifications of a canceled wedding, they had time before they dug that deep.

But they were here together now. "You're crazy," she muttered.

He grinned. "Can't say I haven't thought the same thing myself after yesterday. But in that moment, I couldn't stand by and lose you forever." He rose to his feet, picked up the tray, and put it back on the table, returning to her side of the bed and sitting down beside her.

He grasped her hand, holding her palm in his. "I always considered you mine, even after I let you go. I just didn't let myself go there again."

She saw the truth swirling in the green depths of his eyes, and she was forced to ask the question she'd wanted to put off, the one that had always haunted her. "Why didn't you come to me sooner?"

He shook his head, letting her know it was obviously something he'd thought about before. "Because I'd made my decision to let you go so you could pursue your dreams and live the life you'd planned."

She tilted her head to the side, wondering if she'd heard him wrong. "But I planned my life with you." A life, a future, she'd seen it all in vivid color in her mind… until he'd shattered her dreams.

"But before me you'd wanted to go away to college," he reminded her. "To have time to explore without your brothers always there, and you deserved to have those things. Not to make a choice at seventeen years old that would bind you to me for the rest of your life. I didn't want you to end up resenting me." He glanced at their intertwined hands, then up at her face.

She opened her mouth but he cut her off, placing his finger over her lips. "I know you wouldn't have agreed with me. That's why I made the choice for you," he said.

"You had no right to decide for me." She swallowed over the lump in her throat, a combination of pain and anger, unable to believe that while she'd always thought he'd ended things because he no longer loved her, he'd been looking out for her in his own misguided way. "What about after? Why didn't you come to me after I came back from school?"

He groaned, the sound resigned. "I broke your heart. I devastated you and I didn't think you'd give me another chance. You were dating and I thought you needed to do that, too. Then you met Jason and suddenly things were serious." His thumb brushed over the top of her hand as he paused, deep in thought.

"I told myself it was what I wanted for you, to move on and be happy. I had my feelings for you bottled up so tight I never let myself go there emotionally. But then you walked down that aisle and I really saw you. And realized all I was losing. So when the minister asked if anyone objected, I didn't think, I reacted." He met her gaze, and in that moment, he was the same boy she'd fallen in love with. "I followed my heart and I can't tell you I regret it. I only regret that you were hurt in the process."

She shook her head, the truth as difficult to hear as it was for her to process. "Like I said, Ryder, you're crazy."

"Crazy for you," he said, leaning forward and sealing his lips over hers.

He caught her off guard, but the heat and warmth of his mouth were familiar and surprisingly welcome. His lips moved over hers, his tongue darting inside as he licked, sucked, and devoured her in a way no man but him ever had. His kiss turned hotter, one that stated his intention to possess and stake his claim.

There was no other way to explain it and nothing she could do but grasp his shoulders and hold on for the ride while enjoying every second. He pushed her against the pillows so he could deepen their connection, and her heart pounded against her chest, desire for this man consuming her and forcing her to come to painful conclusions.

Losing Jason had been difficult. Embarrassing. Painful, even. But losing Ryder when she was younger had hurt even more. She'd always wondered what could have been. What could she have done to change the outcome of their relationship? What could their future have been if things had been different?

She never thought she'd have the chance to find out, but here they were. She lifted her hands to his hair and curled her fingers into the long strands, holding him to her, kissing him back as thoroughly and as deeply as he kissed her, until he lifted his head, breathing heavily.

"We're good together, Sierra. And we owe it to ourselves to explore it further. I want to be the man to give you everything you want and need and dream of." He met her gaze. "But it's up to you. In the meantime, I need a cold shower," he muttered before turning and walking away.

Leaving her to decide what happened next.

A few seconds later, the sound of the water turning on and running echoed through the pipes in the room. He was in the bathroom naked, droplets cascading over his well-honed body, soap making his muscles slick and wet.

She laid her head against the pillows and groaned in frustration. She could lie here debating what to do for the next two days she had in this hotel suite, a respite from the insanity and chaos that awaited her at home, or she could do what her body told her it wanted. What her heart had wanted since the day he'd ended things between them.

He'd hurt her once, walked away without warning. What was to prevent him from doing the same thing again? She couldn't ever let herself forget that.

But she'd thought she'd moved on from him enough to marry another man. Clearly, she'd been wrong. Closure was important and she needed to know if her memories were just that or if he was going to forever ruin her for another man and a real future.

If that was the case, God help her.

She might not know what she wanted from life right now, but it had become crystal clear that it wasn't Jason. But she also knew that just because Ryder had stopped her from being with another man didn't mean he automatically fit into the space Jason had left behind.

With that warning firmly in mind, she contemplated exploring this thing between them and putting it to rest once and for all.

# Chapter Three

Lifting the covers off her body, Sierra stood and unhooked her bra, dropping it to the floor, followed by her underwear. Then she drew her courage around her and headed for the bathroom, pushing the door open and stepping into the steam-filled room, her heart racing wildly in her chest at what she was about to do.

Ryder's face was upturned to the water, and she took a second to admire the width of his chest, the hard muscles in his arms, and the way he braced his strong legs, his cock hard and standing upright. He obviously wanted her as much as she wanted him.

Desire didn't scare her. It was the notion of falling hard for him all over again that frightened her. But she'd made her decision. She'd be brave and see where things stood, and right here, right now, she wanted Ryder.

Needed him.

Without waiting for him to notice her, she opened the shower door and stepped in. His eyes opened and flared but he didn't hesitate. He pulled her against him, the hard ridge of his erection nudging against her belly.

She gasped at the feel of him, at the desire that spread through her and lit up her body, as his mouth descended on hers.

Water slid over her but she didn't care, not when he was

devouring her, his tongue delving deep into the back of her mouth, tasting her everywhere as it tangled with hers. With a moan, she wrapped her arms around his neck and gave in to the yearning that was consuming her.

In the past, their time together was often rushed, hidden from adults, stolen moments when they could be together. Today they had all the time in the world or at least as long as the water remained hot, she thought, holding back a laugh.

He gripped her head and tilted her neck, giving him deeper access to her mouth, his lips gliding over hers, back and forth, and she pushed against him, rubbing her aching breasts over his chest.

"God, I missed this. I missed you." His huskily spoken words sent a shiver through her along with a hint of hope that she ruthlessly squashed.

"Tell me," he said, nipping on her bottom lip.

"What?"

"That this isn't just revenge sex. Angry sex. Tell me you want me, too."

Dammit, he was going to dig into her emotions and there was no way to stop it. Because she couldn't deny the truth, and maybe she didn't want to anyway. She'd been denying her feelings for Ryder for way too long, and it was time that she was honest with herself, as well as with him.

"I'm not here because I'm angry or pissed or because I want to get back at Jason for walking away from me. I missed you, too," she admitted.

And she had.

So much it hurt.

"Then take off the bracelet," he said on a growl.

She blinked, looking down at her right wrist, which held a bracelet that Jason had bought her with their initials intertwined. He'd given it to her when their relationship had gotten serious, and she'd been wearing it for so long it had become a part of her. She'd forgotten she still had it on, and she said a silent prayer of thanks Jason's best man had been holding on to her engagement ring along with the wedding band. Ryder's reaction to that wouldn't have been good.

Although she'd made no decisions about her life, she knew things were over with Jason or she wouldn't be here now, with Ryder. She unhooked the bracelet, stepped out of the shower, and put it on the counter, returning to Ryder.

"Done," she said.

With a groan, he slid his hands down her neck and over her breasts, cupping the mounds. She closed her eyes as he plumped her flesh, then pinched her nipples as he pulled, the mix of pain and pleasure shooting straight to her core.

She'd been young when they were together last, and sex had been hot and frenzied so as not to get caught by an adult or so she could rush home for curfew.

She hadn't been his first, though he'd been hers. Another reason she'd fallen so hard so fast for him. He'd been patient and sweet that initial time. But they'd both been inexperienced despite the burning passion between them.

Now he was a man in charge, one who knew how to arouse a woman, and he was taking care of her with an expert touch. He slid his hands through the soap on the shelf, rubbing both palms together before turning his attention back to her breasts, soaping them up while playing with her nipples, alternately pinching then soothing the sting.

Her legs trembled, need pulsing in her core. As if he knew she needed him now, he dropped to his knees, pressing his mouth to her stomach in a reverent kiss.

"Oh God." Just the sight of him kneeling before her had moisture settling between her thighs and her damn heart swelling in her chest.

He glanced up at her, then slid his mouth lower, over her pubic bone and to her bare sex. The anticipation was killing her, made more intense when he slicked his hands up her legs until they settled at her thighs, her body on edge as she waited for whatever he planned next.

He licked over her sex and she leaned back, her head hitting the wall.

"I'd forgotten how good you taste," he said, following that erotic comment up with another teasing glide of his tongue. "I'm going to rectify that," he murmured, then began to eat at her like a starving man devouring his last meal.

She had nothing to hold on to as he slid his tongue over her lips, nipping and licking over and over before thrusting it into her body. She whimpered at the slick invasion, shocked when he began to circle her clit with one thumb.

Her fingers curled into his hair as he worked her into a frenzy, her orgasm building fast as she came with a cry, her body not her own as waves of pleasure overtook her.

Coming back to herself, she realized he'd stood up and she looked into his satisfied expression. "Pleased with yourself?" she asked.

"Quite," he said with a grin.

Glancing down, she saw his cock hard and erect, in need of attention. She reached between them, wrapping her hand around his velvety thickness.

He grasped her wrist and pulled her off. "I'm not coming unless I'm inside you."

She moaned her frustration. "Why don't the same rules apply to us both?" she asked as he slipped his fingers between her lower lips once more.

To her surprise, her hips bucked greedily, as they sought out harder contact, more friction.

He chuckled at her clearly mixed message. "Because I'm in charge, sweetheart."

And as his finger pinched her clit, she couldn't bring herself to argue the point.

"This pussy's mine, baby. Nobody else's," he said as he slid one finger inside her, then another.

"Oh God."

"Am I right? Nobody's ever worked you up like this?" he

asked, not mentioning anyone else by name, but Sierra knew he was staking his claim. And why.

And as he hooked his finger, gliding the pad over her G-spot, she felt as if he owned her. Her legs trembled, her body shaking as a need to climax built inside her. He knew just where to touch her and how. He rubbed over the spot inside her while holding her upright with one hand around her waist.

"Tell me or else." He stopped all movement, gliding his fingers out of her body.

"It's yours. Only you can get me this hot. Now don't stop," she implored him, and he immediately reinserted both fingers into her body, pressing, gliding in and out, taking her higher.

Before she knew it, she was coming, the waves of rapture rushing through her and consuming her whole. As she returned to herself, he was kissing her, rubbing his cock against her.

She moaned, arching into him, needing to feel him inside her.

"We need to talk," he said, meeting her gaze. "I don't have any condoms. It's not like I came prepared for this. And I've never not used one."

She looked into his familiar green eyes, and in this, she trusted him. "I'm on the pill. And I've never had sex without one."

"I swear to you, neither have I."

She reached for his shoulders, but he grasped her hips and spun her around. "Hands on the wall."

He was a different man than the boy she used to sleep with, she thought, enjoying everything he did to her body. Without hesitation, she braced her hands against the tile, her ass out.

He eased her legs apart and slid his fingers over her, slicking her own juices around her body. Then his thick cock grazed her entrance. She gasped at the size of him, closing her eyes and groaning at the delicious invasion. He shoved in deep, his back covering hers as he paused for a long while.

"What's wrong?" she asked when he paused and waited.

His lips grazed her neck, licking, nibbling, and kissing her. "I'm just savoring the moment," he said in a deep voice, made rough by emotion.

Her heart cracked at the admission, the words meaning something deep in her heart. The heart she'd sworn to protect.

And then he started to move again and she wasn't thinking about anything except maintaining her hold on the wall and the way he filled her up, thick and hard. With his grip on her waist, he pounded into her, taking everything and giving back at the same time.

"Ryder, Ryder, Ryder," she chanted in time to his thrusts. "I'm so close."

"Damn, my name on your lips sounds like heaven," he muttered. "Wait for me," he said, followed by increasingly faster shifts of his hips.

She held on, whimpering, until he groaned. "Now, sweetheart."

She gasped, released everything she'd been holding back, and screamed as she came, feeling him swell and pulse inside her as he climaxed along with her.

Her legs shook and she wasn't even aware when he turned her around and eased her down on the stone seat in the shower. The water had cooled and he moved quickly, soaping up his hands and rinsing them both off.

She was a boneless mess as he cleaned them both up, shut off the shower, and wrapped her in a fluffy white towel.

He dried her off, then slid the hotel robe around her body. By then she was able to help get herself together. He dried himself quickly and picked her up in his arms, striding back to the bed. He stripped her of the robe, and they crawled back under the covers, where she proceeded to crash hard.

* * * *

Ryder couldn't fall back to sleep. Not after what had just happened in the shower with Sierra. He wanted a second chance. Not because the sex was spectacular, which it was, but because this woman was the very best part of him.

As much as he, his father and brother, had been a tight-knit family after his mother died when Ryder had been thirteen, it had taken being with Sierra to fill that missing piece and make him whole.

After he'd ended things, he'd more than missed her but he'd had to let her go. He'd had no choice but to move on with his life, and sure, there had been other women, but he'd already had the best and none after had been her. None lived up to her memory, so he'd never gotten close with anyone else, never considered a future with any other female.

As he'd told her, he hadn't let himself think about going back to her, but now that he thought about it, maybe a part of him had been holding on to the past, hoping for another chance with her. Something had kept him from moving on completely.

She, on the other hand, had had no choice but to believe they were over for good. He'd given her no reason to think they could have anything ever again. She'd been so hurt, she'd avoided him when his relationship with her brother brought them together. She'd had boyfriends who came and went. And then she'd found Jason, a good man, but she hadn't been in love with him. Something inside Ryder's chest had loosened when he'd heard that, learned she'd had second thoughts.

He might have objected as a spur-of-the-moment decision, the fear of losing her forever suddenly stark and clear. But when they'd been in the car, his understanding had crystallized, along with his determination to see if what they had was still real.

By this morning, he knew what he wanted.

And when she'd joined him in the shower? A purely primal need to claim her had overtaken him. He'd never experienced a moment like that with a woman ever before in his life.

He didn't think that just because he'd explained himself, she'd fall into his arms and they could go forward together. She was sweet and sensitive and he'd bruised her heart. He'd also proven himself to be unreliable when it came to his staying power. Which left him in the unenviable position of having to win her all over again.

Because he had every intention of keeping her, this time for good.

* * * *

Since Ryder was the only one with pants and a shirt to put on, he went to the shops downstairs and bought everything he could think of that they might need. Most of the clothing included resort logos, which he didn't think Sierra would be too fond of but he found amusing.

The weather in Pennsylvania was warm for this time of year, so he picked out tank tops, T-shirts, shorts, and sweat pants for later on when the sun went down. He added bathing suits, knowing Sierra was going to strangle him for his choice for her. He shrugged. Next time she could go shopping for them, he thought wryly. He even found resort-themed flip-flops so they didn't have to wear their dress shoes. All in all, he was pretty impressed with himself.

While in the lobby, he looked into the resort's offerings for things to do while they were in the Poconos. The hotel and its neighboring resort events were booked thanks to it being the end of May and the beginning of the late spring-early summer season. But there was a small bay trip that had been booked by a couple who had apparently had an argument and abruptly canceled their reservation.

Ryder was able to order a picnic basket filled with lunch and Prosecco, a golf cart that he could use to drive them to their destination, and thanks to the fact that the water rides were open and full, they might even find time and space to be alone.

He was walking back to the room when his cell rang. He pulled it out of his pocket and glanced at the screen, hitting answer.

"Sebastian." He wasn't shocked to hear from Sierra's brother.

The man might be Ryder's best friend, but his first concern was always going to be his sister. As it should be, Ryder thought. He had no doubt Sebastian was making the call because he was the closest to Ryder, but Ethan and Parker were probably right there, breathing down his neck, waiting for answers.

"Hey, man. Everything okay?" Sebastian asked.

"Everything's fine. Sierra's okay," Ryder said, reassuring his friend. He stopped by a tree outside and spoke quietly and in private.

"Is she? Because she was supposed to be married and on her way to her honeymoon right now."

He glanced up at the blue sky. "She left with me willingly. I didn't kidnap her or anything. We're... working through things." Ryder blew out a breath, knowing he had to tread carefully.

His personal relationship and what he did with Sierra was none of her brothers' business, even if her well-being was.

"Can I talk to her?" Sebastian asked.

"I'm not in the room right now, but I'll let her know you called, and if she wants to get in touch, she will."

A few beats passed before Sebastian spoke again. "You hurt her badly once. I know you had your reasons and I was torn by what you did, but I understood it. But if you aren't in this for keeps, Ryder, bring her the hell home now."

"I'm in it deep." He just wasn't sure whether or not she was. "Have you heard from Jason?" He forced out the name because he needed to know if the man had had a change of heart, wanting to find and talk to his almost-bride.

"No."

Ryder heard the anger in that one word, and though the news came as a relief to him, he knew it was going to hurt Sierra to know the man hadn't come after her. Unless she asked, he had no intention of telling her and rubbing salt in an open wound. One Ryder, himself, had created.

"I didn't handle it well but I know what I'm doing," he said to his friend. He was trying to win the girl.

"I hope so," Sebastian said. "I'll talk to you soon."

"Yeah." He disconnected the call and Ryder shoved his phone back into his pocket, pushing away thoughts of Sierra's groom.

He clearly had no place in her life.

But Ryder wasn't ready to think about what the future held for them. After coming together in the shower, they'd silently agreed to drop the heavy conversation and just enjoy the time they had here. He could tell from her change in mood and how she'd relaxed that she wasn't dwelling on yesterday, the wedding, or anything they'd discussed about the past.

The time would come when they'd have to deal with leaving here and whatever the future held. But while he had the chance, he had every intention of finding his way back into her heart.

He arrived back at the room, bags in hand, to find Sierra sitting with the hotel robe wrapped around her, thumbing through a resort magazine.

She glanced up as he walked in the door, excitement in her expression as she eyed the packages. "What did you get?" she asked, tossing the magazine onto the other side of the bed.

"A lot of clothing with Paradise Cove logos on it." He tossed the white plastic bags onto the mattress. "But the good news is, we have plans for today. A picnic on a small bay near a lake."

She raised her eyebrows at that. "And what are we wearing there?"

"Bathing suits."

She narrowed her gaze. "Oh, really? And how did you know my size for that?"

"Guesswork based on how you fill my hands," he muttered. "It'll be fine. We should be alone. Let's just get changed." He opened one bag, then another, pulling out his shorts so he could change.

Knowing he was in for it when she saw her bathing suit, he grabbed his clothes and headed for the bathroom, closing the door as she yelled.

"I'm not leaving the room in this!"

He winced. Manning up, he returned to face her. "Come on, it's not that bad."

"It's nonexistent, that's what it is!" She held up the tiny red bikini for him to see. Not that he'd been able to get the idea of her wearing it out of his mind since he'd seen the suit on the mannequin in the store.

He couldn't help the grin lifting the edges of his mouth. "Wear it for me?"

Her gaze softened at the request. "Here in the room, yes." She pointed to the spa tub. "Not out in public."

"When we use that tub, you're going to be naked," he told her. This time those blue eyes of hers darkened with need. "Come on. Just change into it and let's enjoy the day." He used his best cajoling tone.

Frowning at him, she snatched up the suit and stormed past him into the bathroom.

He chuckled, calling out, "You might need help with some of the ties!"

She cursed at him from behind the door.

A few minutes later, he'd changed into the shorts and slipped on his shirt just as she walked out of the bathroom in the bathing suit he'd chosen.

He nearly swallowed his tongue at the gorgeous sight. Despite her concerns, the top of the suit had a ruffle over her breasts but her ample cleavage was evident above the edging. She held the sides together with her arms, the strings dangling in the back. And the bottom was a sleek triangle that left little to the imagination and had his mouth watering.

"Turn around and I'll help you." He made a pivoting motion with his finger.

"No." Her eyes flashed icy fire at him.

"You're going with it untied?"

She shook her head. "I'm not going."

He bit the inside of his cheek. "Turn. Around."

"Fine!" She spun one hundred and eighty degrees, giving him

a look at her sleek back... and the globes of her ass.

His cock throbbed inside his shorts. He'd be lucky if they made it out of this room. "You look edible," he murmured, cupping his hand over one cheek and squeezing the bare skin.

She sucked in a startled breath. "You can't really expect me to go out in this."

"I can." He reached for the strings and tied the back of the suit into a tight bow. "And I do. You look amazing and the girl at the desk promised me we'd be alone. They're fully booked at a concert on the pier. It'll be fine." He leaned in close and pressed a kiss to the flesh between her neck and shoulder.

A full-body tremor shook her frame. "Ryder," she said in a husky voice.

"Sierra. Come on a picnic with me. You won't be disappointed. I promise."

* * * *

Thank goodness Ryder had bought a tank top dress for her to wear over the bathing suit. Red, in the resort colors, with the white Paradise Cove logo above her breast. Sierra didn't care because her ass cheeks were now covered.

She walked beside him and he took her hand. She couldn't help but notice how good her hand felt in his bigger one. How right. She pushed those thoughts aside and focused on where they were heading. They approached the far side of the resort, where he gave his name and a golf cart was waiting for them.

The man in charge handed him a resort map and indicated where their destination was by drawing a circle with a magic marker. "Basically follow this path until you reach the bay," the older gentleman said.

"Thank you." Ryder tipped him before helping Sierra into the passenger side of the cart.

He walked around, joining her, and soon they were off.

The sun beat down overhead, but the covered cart protected

her skin. And when she'd packed a bag for the day, she saw that Ryder had bought them sunscreen, too. She'd noticed a picnic basket and ice bucket in the back of the cart, and she had a feeling he'd thought of everything for this little trip.

She glanced at his profile, his face covered in sexy scruff, a Paradise Cove baseball cap backwards on his head. His facial features were relaxed as he maneuvered the cart with one hand.

Considering all they'd been through in the last twenty-four hours, it was amazing they were here. Together. She couldn't say she didn't want to be here, and that scared her.

"Looks like this is it," he said, pulling the cart up to the edge of the path and parking it.

She'd been lost in studying his handsome face, she thought, as she turned to look at the scenery in front of her. Sun danced over the water. The sky was clear, the temperature warm. It was a beautiful day, and she was glad he'd dragged her kicking and screaming here. She knew they couldn't go into the lake. Although it was hot today, the temperature hadn't been consistently warm enough for the water to be comfortable for a dip.

Together they carried supplies from the back of the cart to a place on the shore. They spread out a large blanket, put the picnic basket on it along with a cooler that, it turned out, contained Prosecco on ice.

Then they settled down on the blanket. She opened the basket and began taking out the assortment of food the resort had supplied. Everything from sandwiches to cheese and crackers, strawberries dipped in chocolate, and the wine.

"Sebastian called me earlier," Ryder said, as he opened the bottle and poured the liquid into plastic cups.

He handed her one and she took a long, bubbly sip. "I know what he wanted. What did you tell him?"

Ryder glanced at her. "That you were fine. And here of your own free will."

Her lips curved into a smile. "Poor Sebastian. He must feel like he's in the middle of something he doesn't understand."

Ryder shook his head. "He's not in the middle. He's all Team Sierra. If I hurt you again, he'll kick my ass and not think twice."

"He's a good big brother. But he's also your friend. You know that. Even after you broke up with me, you two stayed close." As she spoke, the truth dawned on her. "Sebastian knew why you ended things, didn't he? And he let me cry over you, knowing your feelings for me hadn't changed?" she asked, her voice rising. "That's not Team Sierra all the way."

He took a large gulp of the drink, too. "Yes, it was. He wanted you to go away to school because it's what you always said you wanted. He didn't want you to have any regrets in your life, either. He was torn but he thought he was protecting you."

She shook her head in frustration. "Why the hell don't the men in my life think I can make decisions for myself?"

"You were too young to know what was best. And honestly, we can't go back and change the past, so we have no choice but to live with it and move forward. Like we had started to. Can we do that?" He lifted his hat off his head, adjusted it, and slid it back on again.

She drew a deep breath, knowing he was right. "I'm trying."

But there was a huge issue of the trust that had been destroyed in his making decisions for her and behind her back at the same time. His willingness to hurt her to give her what he thought she needed. That frightened her.

"That's all I can ask," he said, sounding and looking relieved.

Another question ran through her mind. "Did he say if Jason reached out?" She hated bringing him between her and Ryder, but she had to know.

Ryder shook his head. "He hasn't heard from him. None of your brothers have." He set his jaw, then said, "I'm sorry."

"You didn't stop him from trying to talk to me." Or from picking up where they'd left off in the ceremony, which she had asked him to do.

As much as she hated to admit it, Jason had done her a favor by walking out. She'd been settling, and by extension, so had he.

As angry and hurt as she was, a part of her was coming to understand the way things had played out yesterday. Not that she wanted to dwell on it now. She'd promised herself these two days of respite and she planned to take them.

She breathed in deeply, then exhaled in an attempt to let the negative energy go.

"Take off your dress and let's relax in the sun."

She rolled her eyes. "You're pretty focused on seeing me in that bikini."

He pulled off his shirt and tossed it on the edge of the blanket, drawing her gaze to his tanned, well-muscled chest. "You look pretty focused, too."

She couldn't help it. She laughed as he broke the lingering tension.

Although they weren't totally alone—a few couples were far away on their own spots around the lake—she knew nobody was paying attention to what she and Ryder were doing, too wrapped up in each other to pay attention to anyone else.

She shifted to her knees, lifting the dress, easing it off her head, and placing it on top of his tee.

He patted his lap. "Lie down and let's chill."

Scooting forward, aware of her skimpy suit, she positioned herself until she could place her head in his lap and stretch the rest of her body out on the blanket. She inhaled and took in his now familiar scent, the heat of the sun feeling good against her skin, and she sighed with pleasure.

"Remember when we used to do this under the big tree in your yard?" he asked, looking down at her.

She nodded. "It was hard to find places where we could be alone. Even there I was never sure one of my brothers wasn't looking out a window, watching."

He laughed. "I'm glad I just have an older brother. No sisters to worry about."

"How is Andrew?" she asked.

"Still a workaholic. Still looking for a woman able to tolerate him."

His lips lifted in a grin and she knew he was kidding. He'd always been able to joke about his stuffy older sibling. But they both knew it was thanks to Andrew that Ryder hadn't just stayed home to work at his father's business but had gotten his degrees.

"And your dad?" she asked.

"Retirement is good for him. Good for his heart. So is Elsa, his next-door neighbor in Florida, where he moved. They're together without living together."

She smiled. "Cute. I'm glad everyone is well in your family."

"What about you?" he asked. "I know how your brothers are, of course, but how are you? How's work? Are you happy?"

Her job as the head of the Social Media Division for Knight Time Technology made her happy. "I love the work. I appreciate being able to contribute to the family business by doing something I not only love but I'm good at. It's fulfilling. And I have a good staff and friends. So my work life is great. Personally, family-wise, it's been tough."

"Ethan," he said and she nodded.

"It was hard, him losing his wife that way. And when Sebastian and Ashley went to San Francisco to figure out some company issues, they ended up asking me to do some digging— and I'm the one who found out Mandy had been cheating on Ethan." Her heart squeezed hard in her chest.

She hated that her brother was so unhappy. As the unofficial head of the family, he took care of everyone else, and he deserved more from life than he'd gotten so far.

Ryder squeezed her bare shoulder in support. "Ethan's tough. He'll come out on the other side."

"Eventually, I hope," she murmured, as she relaxed into his lap.

Ryder reached over and picked up a strawberry, its bottom covered in chocolate. "Hungry?" he asked.

"For chocolate? Always."

He grinned and held the small piece of fruit over her mouth so she could take a bite. "Mmm," she said as the mixed sweet and sour flavor exploded on her tongue.

"Does it taste good?"

"Mmm-hmm."

He dipped his finger into the wineglass and ran it over her lips. She slid her tongue out and licked her mouth, catching his fingertip, too. She sucked the liquid off him, watching above her as his gaze darkened with unmistakable need. And beneath her head, his erection swelled and thickened. She felt the arousal in her own body, her breasts suddenly heavy, a slick pulsing between her thighs.

She wasn't surprised when he tossed his hat and leaned his head down, his lips pressing hard against hers.

# Chapter Four

Ryder kissed her, not caring about their awkward angle, taking in her sweet taste and wanting more. He needed to touch her, so he cupped his hand around her neck, then glided his fingers over her collarbone, feeling her delicate body beneath his hands. With a groan, he continued his exploration, dipping his fingers along the neckline of her bathing suit top, the pads grazing the swell of her breasts.

She shivered and her nipples puckered into tight buds, making his mouth water. He shifted her so she was lying on her side instead of straight out in front of him, giving him easier access to slide his hand where he wanted. And what he wanted was to touch every inch of her he could on his path down to her pussy.

He moved his hand, ignoring her breasts, another destination in mind. He splayed his hand across her stomach and she moaned, obviously enjoying it.

*Mine*, he thought.

Not wanting to freak her out completely, he kept the feeling to himself. When he'd gone to the church yesterday, he'd had no idea he'd be here with her today, trying to cement his place in her life. But with his hand possessively on her belly, he had a vision of her pregnant with his child. He swayed, suddenly dizzy, in shock at the course his thoughts had taken. But with everything inside him, it felt right.

She felt right, not just to the touch but to the emotions swirling inside him.

"Ryder?" she murmured. "Is everything okay?"

He glanced down at her, taking in the freckles on her nose, and grinned. "Couldn't be better. I just like the feel of you beneath my hand."

"Mmm," she said, closing her eyes. "I like it, too."

He shifted his stare to his tanned hand against her paler stomach and swallowed back a groan.

With her pleasure as his sole focus, he slipped his fingers beneath her bathing suit and she jumped in surprise.

"Shh. Let me play." Her sex was bare, which turned him the fuck on. He ran his fingers over her pubic bone and lower still, finding her pussy wet for him.

Her eyes flew open, her gaze coming to his, a hazy sheen covering the blue, as desire took hold. "We're outside," she said in a husky voice.

"And at a couples resort and nobody is anywhere near us," he reassured her.

Using two fingers, he slid her juices over her sex, keeping his touch away from where she needed him most. He teased her, arousing her until her hips were rotating in circles, gyrating, low moans coming from deep in her throat.

"Ryder, make me come." She begged him, both in words and with her body's reaction to his fingers, which dipped and played around and around.

Still not touching her clit, he slid one finger inside her and she gasped as he filled her. "Feel good, sweetheart?"

"Oh God. Good but not enough to get me over." She arched her back in silent supplication.

He wiggled her bottoms lower on her thighs so he could pump his finger in and out of her body, her inner walls clasping him in tight, wet heat. His dick was so hard he thought he might come from giving her an orgasm alone.

As he worked her with his finger, he finally gave her what she needed, circling his thumb over the tiny, hard nub that was practically begging for his attention. And if they weren't outside, as she'd pointed out, he'd lift her hips to his face and suck on her until she came. Saving that for later, when they were alone in bed, he pressed hard against her clit, his finger shifting inside her, pressing on her spongy inner walls.

She stiffened at the sudden pressure and began rocking against his hand. "Oh, oh, God, Ryder, I'm coming."

He didn't stop, keeping up both movements as she flew, his gaze on her beautiful face the entire time.

And as she climaxed, her body shook, trembled, grasping his finger, the sight a gorgeous one to behold.

She collapsed onto the blanket, her breath shallow, a fine sheen of sweat glistening on her skin.

"I died and went to heaven," she muttered, pushing herself to a sitting position and glancing directly at his lap, where his cock was hard and evident against his bathing suit shorts.

"What about you?"

"Nothing we can do about it out here. Talk to me about something else. Anything else to distract me."

"Umm–" She obviously searched for something to discuss, but she didn't tear her stare from his erection.

"And stop looking at my cock," he told her. "Or we are going to give those people on the far side of the lake a show."

Her eyes opened wide and she leaned over, opened the picnic basket, and took out food. "Let's eat," she said, her cheeks flushed as she handed him what looked like a chicken sandwich.

He shook his head and laughed. "Can't say I'm hungry for food but yeah. Let's eat."

They chowed down on the contents of the basket, Ryder discovering he was starving after all. Sierra talked about her job, how she was thinking of expanding her social media services to companies beyond Knight Time Technology because she had the time. She even discussed opening her own business so she could work part time from home.

They talked about how his father's business had grown since he'd retired. Ryder and his brother, Andrew, had grown the construction business, expanding into luxury homes. The kind of home he'd like them to live in together one day.

He found himself thinking about the future and things they'd once talked about a long time ago.

"Do you still want a dog?" he asked.

"I do. But working from the office and living in an apartment makes getting one difficult. And besides, I don't want a smaller one. No matter how cute, I'm afraid they'll be loud and yappy."

He grinned. Yet another thing they were on the same page about. He'd love nothing more than a big-ass dog like a Newfoundland or a St. Bernard hanging around the house he'd already built and lived in alone.

Assuming he got the girl.

"What about you?" she asked. "Still want a huge dog?"

"I do." He met her gaze, his voice serious as he said, "I want it all. The family, kids, dog, wife, house… everything we dreamed of."

Her eyes opened wide and a visible tremor shook her. "It's getting late. We should get back," she murmured and started to pack up their picnic.

He told himself not to be discouraged by her reaction, that she had a lot going on her mind and more going on in her personal life that had to be dealt with than he did.

Ryder didn't believe in love at first sight, and in no way was that what they'd experienced. They'd built a relationship, piece by piece, despite the fact that they'd been young and inexperienced in life and love. He was close to her siblings, they shared a love of family, and had wanted the same things out of life. He'd loved everything about her, from her generous personality to the way she'd naturally given him what he needed emotionally, making it easy to return the same.

He'd loved her then. He loved her now and he didn't want to lose her again.

With a muttered curse at the way she'd closed down emotionally, he loaded the golf cart up again.

They drove back to the resort and returned the items. He took heart in the fact that she let him hold her hand as they walked back to their room, and when they stepped inside, he was surprised by what awaited them.

The suite had been cleaned and the shades pulled down. Fake candles were lit around the living room and along the stairs leading up to the hot tub. A champagne bucket sat by a large cheese-and-cracker platter on the table. Rose petals lined the floor leading to the bedroom, where white washcloth swans had been created and sat, intertwined, on the red bed.

"Wow, this is incredible," Sierra said, happiness in her tone as she glanced around. "And the hot tub looks inviting," she murmured.

"Does it?" he asked, imagining them inside it.

"It does." With a twinkle in her gaze, she pulled her dress off and immediately removed her bathing suit. Next, she slid off her flip-flops. Then she turned and walked toward the stairs, giving him an amazing view of her from behind.

He adjusted himself, squeezing his cock tight in warning to behave. It wasn't time. Yet.

Glancing over her shoulder, she crooked her finger at him. "Aren't you going to join me?"

She didn't have to ask twice. He dropped his shorts, removed his shirt, kicked off his flip-flops, and followed her up.

When he joined her in the hot tub, she was playful and eager, kissing him as she grasped his shoulders and lowered herself onto his eager cock.

Whatever was going on with her emotions, sexually she was all in, and they spent the rest of the late afternoon together in the Jacuzzi and the later part of the evening and night enjoying the luxuries provided by the hotel.

The only drawback to the entire day was the emotional separation he knew was between them. He wished he was privy to what she was thinking, where her head was when it came to them and the future.

But she was keeping her feelings close, and his gut told him it wasn't the right time to ask.

\* \* \* \*

Sierra woke up the next morning to an orgasm building inside her that wasn't a dream. One thing she'd learned about Ryder as a man, he was a generous lover, always giving to her, not caring if he received in return. Of course, she always tried, but he was demanding, wanting to come inside "his" pussy, as he'd declared her private parts last night.

He loved oral sex, which in turn had, in two short days, taught her to love oral. He hadn't yet let himself finish in her mouth, but he thoroughly enjoyed what she did to him before he slammed inside her and made her come so hard she saw stars.

No one could say they weren't sexually compatible, she thought, as his mouth worked on her now. She arched her back, and unable not to, she ground herself against him as his tongue slid in and out of her sex, his teeth alternately grazing her clit.

Her climax, when it hit, was as explosive as usual with Ryder, sending her soaring. And when she came back down to earth, it was to the sight of him rubbing his mouth on her thigh with a grin.

"Good morning, sweetheart."

"Good morning." She smiled back, but neither the incredible orgasm nor his easy, sexy smile could prevent the unwelcome anxiety that balled in the pit of her stomach. Because it was the morning of their second day.

The end of their retreat.

Time to return to reality and everything that waited for her. She had to face the people she'd left behind when she'd willingly run away from her wedding with the man who wasn't her groom.

"Talk to me," Ryder said as he slid up beside her and pulled her into his arms. "I saw the minute your mind turned back on."

She rubbed her eyes, which had stupid tears forming. "It's time to go home."

"It is." His jaw pulled tight. "But that doesn't have to mean the end of us." He threaded their fingers together in a show of unity she wasn't sure she could reciprocate. "I understand that just two days ago you were engaged to another man." He paused, then said, "But he let you go."

"He did. But that doesn't mean I'm—"

"I love you, Sierra."

The words she hadn't heard in years seemed to echo around her. Words she'd come to believe were a lie because, if he'd loved her, he wouldn't have left her.

"I have always loved you," Ryder went on, not waiting for her to reply. "I just shoved the feelings away so you could go on with your life. The time wasn't right then but it can be now."

She glanced at their entwined hands. "Do you have any idea how much you hurt me back then?"

His silence told her that he did. Or at least, now he knew.

"You took all my hopes and dreams and crushed them because you decided you knew what was best for me. That just because I once wanted to go away to college, I couldn't change my mind. You didn't trust in me, the things I told you I wanted, the hopes and dreams I spun for us… You let them all go."

"I—"

"I'm not finished," she said, staring at the blank television screen across from the bed, not looking at him as she let all the feelings of the past spill forth. "You let me think you didn't love me anymore, and I know you dated other women after me. Of course you did." The pain of that sliced through her as if it were fresh and new.

"None were you," he said so low she had to lean close to hear.

So close she smelled his natural scent and wanted to burrow into his embrace. But she couldn't because that would be cowardly.

Dealing with her life, then being alone were both brave and necessary. "I need to go home, Ryder. I need to talk to Jason. We need closure."

"I don't like it," he muttered.

She didn't laugh at his petulant tone. "You don't have to. That's just the way it is. And I need time to think." About them, she thought, letting the words go unsaid.

"I said I don't like it but I didn't say I don't understand it." He sat up, jarring her because she'd been leaning against him.

The next thing she knew, she was on her back on the mattress and he was looming over her, his hands on either side of her shoulders, his big body warm and tempting above her. Those beautiful green eyes stared into hers, and she saw the truth in their depths. He loved her now. And she was very much afraid she loved him, too.

But she wasn't ready. Just because she was suddenly single didn't mean she could make decisions about another relationship or commitments to a man who'd once pushed her away.

"Ryder—"

He shook his head. "No more talking. I'm going to take you home and give you what you say you need. But I'm going to give you one last thing to remember me by before you go," he said before his lips descended on hers.

Her hands came to his head, sifting through the silken strands, holding him tight as he kissed her. Wanting him with every fiber of her being.

Unlike many of their moments together here, this wasn't the frenzied, hot and heavy sex she'd gotten used to. The kind with the fire that burned out of control. This was slow and sensual. As if he wanted her to feel every glide of his lips, every stroke of his tongue, and memorize the sensations.

She knew she'd never forget. He was gentle as he made love to her mouth, slowly relearning all the spots inside that were made just for him. He kissed her like that for what felt like hours, reminding her of the times when they were younger. When they knew they couldn't go further but they could kiss and make out and he could grind himself against her, and it was hotter than the sexual act itself.

His thick erection slid over and over her sex, gliding against her clit, rocking her ever so slowly to orgasm. She'd forgotten what these kinds of make-out sessions were like. The sweet intensity. The deep kisses. Hands moving everywhere. And hips rotating over and over until the heavy waves came at her almost out of nowhere, then consumed her.

"Oh God, coming, coming, I'm coming," she whispered on a ragged moan, the hard press of his cock thrusting against her sex.

Only when she'd succumbed to her last tremble did Ryder speak. "Eyes on me, sweetheart."

She hadn't realized she'd closed them. Forcing her heavy lids open, she met his gaze.

Desire flashed in the depths of his eyes. "I want you to know who's making love to you," he said as he notched himself at her entrance, then slowly, deliberately thrust in deep.

Her eyes opened wider as he took her completely, filling her up, both her body and her heart. Damn him, she thought, tears threatening. She didn't want to cry at how good they were together. She couldn't do that and leave.

But she was going to leave him. She had to figure things out alone.

"Stop thinking." Arms braced on either side of her shoulders, he raised his hips, and she shuddered, aware of every inch of his velvety length as he pulled out of her, then shoved back in. "Feel us, Sierra."

She couldn't do anything but feel as he thrust in and out, over and over. But before she could even start to build toward a climax, he stopped and pushed himself to a sitting position, taking him with her.

"What are you doing?"

"Making you feel."

And then they were rocking together, face to face, eye to eye as he hit her clit with every roll of his hips against hers. It was sweet and emotional, the waves building as he made love to her, slowly and deliberately taking them both up and over.

And when she came, his hands were in her hair, pulling her into him, sealing his lips over hers as the pulsing of his erection and the low, satisfied groan told her he came, too.

They came together.

\* \* \* \*

The ride home was silent. Ryder left Sierra alone with her thoughts, knowing his words had already come from the heart and his actions had left her with no lingering doubt about how he felt. He loved her. He wanted to spend the rest of his life with her.

But she'd made her feelings clear, too. She needed time. So they had packed their wedding clothes and extra resort wear, pulling things together and using extra laundry bags from the hotel to put their resort clothing in. He'd tossed everything into the trunk and off they went.

He drove her to the apartment building where she and her brothers resided. The place itself was owned by Knight Time Technology and all the siblings lived in separate apartments in the building. Sebastian with his wife, Ashley, Ethan, alone now that Mandy was gone, and Parker.

Sierra, he knew, had packed her things to officially move in with Jason after they returned from their honeymoon. She was going home to big boxes and everything unsettled.

He hated it.

He wanted to be there to make things easier for her, but she'd insisted that she was going home alone. That they weren't returning as a couple.

Fine.

He could accept what she wanted for now, but that didn't mean he was leaving her to deal with the shit storm he'd caused and she'd left behind.

For tonight, he walked her up to her door, making sure she got home safely, and kissed her good night—a long, lingering, sizzling kiss that hopefully would keep her tossing and turning all night long.

Then he went home alone to think.

And to plan.

\* \* \* \*

Sierra stared at the taped-up boxes that filled her living room and wanted to cry at the sight. When she'd packed them up, she'd been excited to start her new life. Now she had to undo it all.

Sunlight streamed through the window in the living room, casting a glow directly on the wrapped packages, the gifts from the wedding. Her stomach churned at the sight. Obviously her brothers had decided this was the best place to leave them. Somehow she'd have to return them all. Make sure everyone who'd given her a gift got a refund.

She ran a hand over her eyes, wishing she had her Keurig, but that was packed in a box, along with her coffee pods, sugar, and cups. What she needed was a Starbucks run before tackling anything here, including letting her brothers know she was home.

She grabbed her purse and started for the door when she heard a knock. Oh, no. Ryder must have spoken to Sebastian already, and instead of going to work, he was here to...

What? Lecture her? Hug her?

She swung the door open wide, speaking as she did. "Sebastian, I was going to call— Ryder. What are you doing here?"

He stood at her door wearing a pair of aviator glasses that looked sexy on his face, a backwards ball cap that reminded her of their day on the lake at the Poconos, and food. But she hadn't expected to see him again... well, not until she was ready.

"I come bearing sustenance." He held out a Starbucks bag. "Venti vanilla latte with three extra pumps of syrup and a pumpkin loaf." He dangled the bag as a peace offering.

She narrowed her gaze. "How do you know my order?" Or at least the order she would use on a day she was feeling particularly down.

He shrugged. "I asked your brother."

So he had spoken to Sebastian, which meant she was going to have company times three… four if you counted Ashley, very soon. She hadn't even called her own friends yet, unsure of how to explain what she'd done. It was going to be easier to rationalize why Ryder had interrupted the ceremony than why she'd left with him, she thought, cheeks burning.

Ryder cleared his throat. "Can I come in?"

She stepped aside so he could enter and shut the door behind him, accepting the coffee and bag with the treat. She stepped toward the kitchen and put everything down on the counter.

She turned, realizing he'd followed closely behind. He looked better than she did, his faded jeans and black shirt giving him a sexy appearance, while she wore a clean pair of sweats from the Poconos resort and a T-shirt with a logo on it.

She needed to find the boxes with her clothing. "Why are you here?" she asked again.

"Because you have a lot to do and I want to help you do it." He spread one arm, gesturing to the other room, where the boxes were piled. "After all, it's my fault." He had the good grace to look embarrassed.

She blew out a breath, knowing his coming here was a sweet, thoughtful gesture. "But didn't I say I needed time?" she asked, trying to be gentle but knowing she had to stand firm.

He folded his arms across his chest, his muscles showing beneath his T-shirt. "I didn't say I was going to kiss you. Or fuck you. Or make slow, passionate love to you—although that's all on the table if you just give me the okay."

Now her cheeks were flaming, she thought, as she spun away. "If you want to help me, then thank you." She wasn't going to look a gift horse in the mouth. Besides, he was right. It was his fault she was in this situation. "All my furniture is still here. I need to cancel the movers for next week," she muttered. "But we can open boxes and start putting things away… Oh, damn."

"What's wrong?" he asked.

"The scissors are packed. I have no way to open the boxes."

He frowned. "Tell you what. I'll run to the store and buy scissors so we can get started. You make whatever phone calls you need to make."

"I don't have my phone yet."

Ryder lifted his cap and reset it on his head. "Sebastian said he'd come down this morning, so I'm guessing he'll bring it."

Her eyes opened wide. "Can you be gone when he shows up? It's going to be hard enough to talk to him without you here!"

He shook his head. "I'll go get the scissors. But get used to having me around helping you. That's nonnegotiable," he said, and with a grin, he turned and walked out, leaving her flustered, flabbergasted, and pissed.

She didn't need his help. He'd caused this mess! But it really was nice of him to acknowledge it and want to fix it. *Because he has an agenda! He wants you and this is his way of getting an in!*

She really needed to stop arguing with herself, she mused, as the doorbell rang.

"Sebastian." This time when she opened the door, it was to her brother.

Times three.

# Chapter Five

No sooner had Sierra opened the door than her brothers barged in, one right after the other without waiting to be asked or even saying hello to her first.

"Come in, why don't you," she muttered to herself.

"Jesus Christ, Sierra. I was so fucking worried about you," Ethan said, pulling her into his arms, and her brief flare of frustration with him eased.

She wrapped her arms around his waist and laid her head on his chest as she had many times when she was a little girl and things in her life had gone wrong. He'd always been there for her and she knew he always would be. They all would. For all their overprotective ways, they were wonderful big brothers and she loved them.

"I'm fine," she assured him. Taking a step back, she spun around, a forced smile on her face. "See?"

Sebastian shook his head at her antics.

"You gave us a scare when we came into the room and you were gone," Parker said. "With Ryder."

"He didn't kidnap me," she said, defending Ryder. "I went willingly. And I checked in. I let Sebastian know I was okay."

"Doesn't mean we didn't worry," Sebastian said, holding out

her phone, and she took it gratefully.

"Don't you three have to be at work?" she asked, taking in their dress. They all wore suits meant for the office. Now that they saw she was fine, maybe they'd go without forcing her to talk about things.

Ethan scowled. "Now listen to me, young lady," he said in the tone he'd used when she was a naughty teenager. "Do you really think you're getting off that easy?"

She rolled her eyes, but before she could say anything, Sebastian did. "Lay off, Ethan. She's an adult. She can make her own decisions."

She blew out a relieved breath, glad she had at least one brother on her side. Parker, as usual, said nothing, just watched carefully as things went on around him. Neutral, hence his nickname in the family, Switzerland, she mused. Which also came from his past as an almost-Olympic skier before a career-ending injury prevented him from fulfilling his dream.

"Now tell us what decisions you've made." Sebastian folded his arms across his chest and pinned her with his steady gaze.

"Seriously?" She'd thought he understood her best in this situation, that he was going to give her space. Apparently not. "Listen, guys. I love you and I know you love me. But I didn't walk into that church planning to run away with Ryder. I don't know what I want! Or what I'm even ready for now."

Their gazes softened.

"Do you love him?" Ethan asked. There was no question he was talking about Ryder and not her former groom.

She blew out a long breath, then strode to the window and looked out over Manhattan. With the crowded buildings and the people down below rushing along the sidewalks, it was such a big difference from the wide-open spaces and trees in the Poconos.

Did she love Ryder?

There were different kinds of love, she knew now. She'd loved being with Jason. She enjoyed his company, they had wanted the same things out of life, and she knew he'd give her the family of her own that she wanted.

But Ryder filled her soul. It might be a cheesy movie phrase but he completed her. He was her other half, and she didn't need to dig deep to explain to herself why. It was a fact of life, like breathing.

"I love him," she admitted, saying the words out loud for the first time in forever.

Parker came up behind her and wrapped an arm around her. "Trust yourself," he said, kissing her on the cheek.

"I do. But can I trust him again?" she asked quietly.

Could she believe in Ryder to give her the security she desperately needed? Could she trust him not to get something crazy into his head and make a decision for her that would leave her gutted again?

"You're adults now," Sebastian said. "I told him not to go there with you if he wasn't all in. So for what it's worth, I trust him."

She swallowed the lump in her throat.

"Let me put it to you this way." She turned at the sound of Ethan's voice. "If I were walking you down the aisle to Ryder, I wouldn't stop and ask if you were sure. And I wouldn't worry deep down that you weren't getting every last thing you needed from the man you loved."

Parker stepped forward, taking her hand. "I agree with them, sis. He's a good guy. And it's clear as hell he loves you."

She looked at Sebastian, Ryder's best friend. He knew him better than anyone here.

Her youngest brother nodded his head. "He'll do right by you this time. I know he was trying to do right by you last time... and so was I. I'm sorry I didn't tell you I knew why he ended things. We both thought we knew what was best, and we should have let you make your own decision about what you wanted in life."

She blinked and a tear ran down her face.

"Ryder learned his lesson," he said in a gruff voice. "He loves you and he won't leave you again."

For some reason, hearing it from her brother was something she'd desperately needed. Ryder might have promised the same things, but Sebastian's trust in him took care of the final worry she had.

Was it crazy to contemplate jumping from almost marrying one man straight into the arms of another? Completely insane, she thought. But how could she risk losing him again for the sake of taking time she didn't need?

"I love you guys," she said to her brothers. "And I'm sorry I made you worry."

"Love you, too," they all muttered in their rough, brotherly way.

"What are you going to do?" Ethan asked.

She ran her tongue over her dry lips. "Well, I'm going to find the box marked *clothing* and dig out something normal to wear." She glanced down at the red Paradise Cove sweats she had on. "And then I'm going to go see Jason, talk to him, and return his bracelet."

She had the bracelet sitting on her nightstand. She'd unpacked it first thing, not wanting to misplace it.

"Want me to go with you?" Sebastian offered.

"Any of us?" Ethan asked.

Parker just nodded his agreement.

"No." She rubbed her hands together nervously. "I have to face this on my own. Jason stormed out without talking to me. Is that love? Was he having second thoughts of his own and Ryder just gave him an excuse to walk away?" She gave voice to the questions that she hadn't let herself deal with during her weekend away. "Or was he just embarrassed by the fact that I did turn around to look at Ryder instead of staring at my groom?"

Ethan met her gaze, a warm smile lifting his lips. "When did you grow up on me?" he asked with a chuckle.

Given everything going on in his life lately, she liked hearing the slightest laugh from him.

"I don't know when, but I'm certain it's thanks to you that I'm able to handle this. All of you. You've always been there for me. But now it's time for me to stand on my own two feet."

And that meant facing the man she had been supposed to marry.

\* \* \* \*

Sierra approached Jason's secretary, a woman she not only knew well but who had been at their aborted wedding. Hoping her cheeks weren't as red as they felt, she stopped at the desk.

They'd agreed she'd come to see him at the office. She wondered if it was because he had work to do or because it was less personal to have this conversation here.

"Hi, Claire."

"Sierra. Hi," the other woman said softly, no judgment in her expression. "Mr. Armstrong is expecting you. You can go right in."

Nerves fluttered again in her belly. "Thank you." She stepped around the desk and approached his door. She knocked once and stepped in at the "Come in" she'd received in response.

Jason sat at his desk, standing as she entered the room. He did well and his office décor reflected as much, with a large mahogany desk, a plush leather chair with wood-grain accents, and large paintings of the ocean on the wall beside his diplomas.

"Hi." She clutched her purse tightly in her hand.

"Hi."

Awkwardness surrounded them, so she forced herself to step forward and sit in one of the client chairs across from his desk. Taking her cue, he strode around the desk and seated himself in the chair beside her.

She took in the lines around his bloodshot eyes. "You look tired."

"Didn't sleep much this weekend."

She managed a nod, her throat too full to speak.

"I did a lot of thinking," he said.

"Me, too."

He raised an eyebrow at that and she blushed, glancing away. She didn't want to discuss her time with Ryder with her ex.

"Look, I just want you to know, I had no way of knowing Ryder was going to interrupt the wedding that way."

He cleared his throat. "I don't blame you for that."

But he obviously blamed her for other things, she thought. And maybe rightly so. "I'm sorry I looked at Ryder when I went down the aisle. I didn't mean to. I was taking in everyone and my gaze landed on him."

"And when the preacher asked if anyone objected? Are you sorry for turning to him then?"

She blinked and did her best not to flinch at his harsh tone. She needed to own her actions, to accept responsibility. "I didn't even realize that I had... but yes. Of course I'm sorry."

He shook his head. "Look, I promised myself I wasn't going to fight with you and I'm not. I just... It was embarrassing, Sierra. And it killed me that something inside me knew all along that you belonged to him. That's why I walked out. Not because of anything you did or didn't do that day. But because I was the odd man out at my own wedding. And I shouldn't have been."

Tears filled her eyes. "I showed up at the church wanting to marry you. But I think we can both admit now that it would have been a mistake. That maybe there were second thoughts neither one of us gave voice to before Ryder did it himself."

He drummed his fingers on the arms of the chair before speaking. "I hate this. When I had a chance to get over my anger and embarrassment, I was pissed at myself for walking away and not fighting for you when I had the chance. Maybe if I had, if I'd shown you that I–"

Before he could go on, she shook her head, not wanting him to put himself out there and embarrass himself more. Once Ryder had objected, he'd owned her.

She might not have known it at the time, might have been furious, angry, humiliated, and a million more adjectives she couldn't think of at the moment, but the biggest one was the one she hadn't known at the time.

Relieved.

She'd been relieved he'd spoken up and put a claim on her at last, because she'd never stopped loving him.

"I'm sorry," she said, forcing the words over the painful lump in her throat.

She opened her purse and pulled out the bracelet she'd put in a jewelry bag she'd found during her unpacking. Placing it in his hand, she curled his fingers around the beautiful jewelry she'd been proud to wear.

"Jesus," he muttered. "We can't try?"

"No," she whispered.

"You're with him."

She hoped to be. She hadn't left Ryder with any indication, positive or negative, about what she wanted for the future. She'd needed to come to him with a clear path to the future and an even clearer heart.

"I'm sorry," she said again. "I'll take care of canceling the movers, returning the gifts… anything else that comes up, just let me know." She pushed herself to a standing position and he rose to his feet. "I wish you all the best, Jason. And someday you'll find someone who deserves you."

She turned and walked out, her heart pounding like a drum, dizziness spinning around in her head. God, that was awful. She'd hated hurting him and he hadn't deserved what she put him through.

\* \* \* \*

Ryder sat in his favorite chair in his family room in the small house he'd bought and renovated for himself. The television was off, leaving him to his own thoughts… and they sucked.

He'd spent the afternoon helping Sierra unpack her things and put them away in her drawers and cabinets. When he'd suggested they order in Chinese for dinner, she'd turned to him with an unreadable expression on her face, and his stomach had cramped badly.

"I need to run an errand," she said from where she stood by an empty box in the bedroom.

"What kind of errand?"

She'd begun pulling clothing she'd just unpacked out of the drawers. "I, umm, I texted Jason earlier. I'm going over there to talk."

His stomach had plummeted to the floor at the news. He'd known she wanted to talk to the man face to face, but he hadn't thought she'd rush over there so soon.

"I have to give him his bracelet back," she said softly. "And we have unfinished business to discuss."

Knowing he'd had no choice, he'd nodded and left her to do what she needed to. Without pressure or influence from him.

So here he sat now, alone in the dark, nursing a beer and hating that he didn't know what was going on between them. As much as it pained him, Sierra had been about to marry the man. Could he be having regrets over walking out and want her back?

Fuck. He ran a hand through his hair.

*He* wanted her back, so he couldn't blame Jason if he was feeling the same way. And Ryder had no moral high ground to stand on. He'd dumped her when they were younger, devastating her in the process, leaving her unable to trust him, his words, or promises now.

His doorbell rang so he put the bottle on the side table and headed to answer it. Probably a neighbor, he thought. They were a friendly bunch around here, always stopping by for one reason or another.

He opened the door in time to see a car which had been parked in his driveway pull out and away. In front of him stood Sierra.

She wore a pair of tight black leggings, ballet flats, and a pink shirt molding to her curves. Her long hair fell over her shoulders in disarray, just the way he liked it. She looked good enough to eat.

He blinked. "Well, this is a surprise."

"A good one, I hope? Because I let the Uber driver leave."

He grinned. "Always good to see you, sweetheart." He just wondered what she wanted. She'd taken a car out of the city and to Long Island to visit him.

She pulled her bottom lip between her teeth, telling him she was nervous. "Sebastian gave me your address."

That's right. She'd never been to his place. Never had a reason before now, he thought. "Well, come in. It's small but I've renovated the whole house. Everything is new. I'd love for you to see it."

He was proud of his work in general, but he loved his home, with the high beam wood ceilings and hardwood floors. It also had enough land and room for additions to be put on, should the time come when he needed it. And God, he hoped he needed it soon.

"Did you take care of your errand?" He forced the word out as she entered the house and he shut the door behind her.

"I did." She faced him, her knuckles white, she was gripping her purse so hard. "That part of my life is over."

Relief swept through him. He didn't know what he'd expected, but if he were Jason, he wouldn't have let her go easily. He didn't want or need to know the details unless she offered them. What mattered to him was that she'd ended things for good with her ex and she was here now. With him.

"And then you came to me?" he asked, wondering what was going on in that enigmatic mind of hers.

"I did."

He blew out a harsh breath. "Sweetheart, you're going to have to give me more than two-word answers and explain where we stand."

She laughed nervously. "Right. Well, it's not that easy to just say it."

"I don't know why unless you're here to end things with me, too." Jesus, why the fuck had he even put that idea out there? "I told you what I wanted already. I want our dream. The one we talked about a long time ago." His heart threatened to explode out of his chest.

"The family, kids, dog, wife, house… everything we dreamed of," she said, repeating his words back to him.

"Yes. That."

"With me."

"And nobody else," he said, staring into her blue eyes.

She visibly swallowed hard. "And you won't ever make a decision for me that ends us. Not ever again."

He shook his head. "Not in this lifetime or however many more I have," he said, barely recognizing his gruff voice as he realized he was about to get everything he'd ever wanted or dreamed of. Everything that mattered to him, anyway.

"Okay. Good. Because I want the same things. The family, kids, dog, husband, house… everything we dreamed of… with you."

He didn't hesitate, pause, or think. He swung her into his arms and headed straight for the bedroom, laying her down on his California-king-size bed. For the wife, the kids, and the massive dog he wanted.

The things it appeared, now, he was going to get.

He came down beside her, pulling her into his arms. "Jesus, you know how to nearly drive a guy to insanity. I died a little inside, knowing you were with him."

She slid her hand over his cheek. "I needed to clear the way for us."

"When did you decide there would be an us?" Because as far as he knew, even earlier today, she was hesitant.

"My brothers came to see me when you went out to get scissors. We all talked. And they convinced me you weren't going anywhere this time. And in my heart, I know we're meant to be."

He let out the breath he'd been holding, probably since interrupting her wedding.

She was his.

All fucking his.

She leaned over and pressed her lips to his. With a groan, he came over her, his mouth sealed against hers. He slid his tongue into the depths, possessing her, devouring her, staking a claim that would last forever.

Stripping off their clothes while kissing and laughing wasn't easy but they managed, coming together again, skin against skin. He glided his hands up from her waist, his thumbs brushing the undersides of her breasts.

She moaned at the light touch and he dipped his head, pulling a nipple into his mouth. Her fingers came back to his hair, holding him to her as he licked, nipped, and laved at the distended peak before switching breasts and giving the same attention to the other side.

He lifted his head, looking into those eyes he loved, before raising himself up. He grasped his cock in one hand and slid it over her damp sex. She sucked in a shallow breath, and he did it again, gliding the head over her clit until she arched her hips, seeking harder, deeper contact.

He couldn't wait to be inside her and poised himself at her entrance. Their gazes held as he pushed into her. She locked her arms around his neck, her stare never leaving his, and as he thrust deep, he knew she was with him one hundred percent, finally giving him all of her.

"Mine," he said, groaning, taking her for the first time with total awareness of what they were to each other.

What they would be.

Forever.

\* \* \* \*

Later, when they were both sated, multiple times over, they lay entwined together. Sierra glanced up at the ceiling, noting the skylight above them for the first time.

"You didn't tell me your house was like the Paradise Cove suite," she said, laughing against his chest.

She hadn't yet seen the rest of the house, but the warmth of this room, the vaulted ceilings, the wood... She was in love.

"I didn't even think about it, to be honest. This one has a shade that works on a remote control. I can shut it at night so the sun doesn't wake me in the morning," he said.

"Oh, nice," she murmured. "So close it now so we don't get woken up at dawn," she said on a yawn.

"You're staying?"

She heard the hope in his voice and knew she'd have to work hard to convince him she was here and all in. "Are you kicking me out?" she asked, glancing up at him with a fake pout on her lips.

"Never," he said, reaching for the remote on the nightstand and shutting the shade.

The next morning, Sierra woke Ryder with her mouth around his hard-as-a-rock erection. She had no intention of being told no this time. She was going to take him all the way to the end. She sucked him down until he hit the back of her throat.

He groaned and began to pump his hips, back and forth, until she knew he was close. And if she hadn't sensed it, his tap on her head would have told her. She shook her head, then went about ignoring him until he came with a shout, spilling himself down her throat.

Satisfied now, she rose and slid up beside him, a grin on her face. "Good morning."

"I told you I like coming inside my pussy."

She shook her head, blushing and laughing at him. "It's better for you to get used to it now."

"Get used to what?" He pushed himself up in bed, his hair messed and sexy, just how she liked it.

"That you won't always get your way." She shrugged. "Just a warning. I've been too easy on you until now."

He tilted his head back and chuckled. "Okay, sweetheart. Consider me warned. So how did you sleep?"

"Amazingly good." The best sleep she'd had in forever, she thought, snuggling into him.

"So when are you moving in?" he asked.

"What?" She sat upright in bed.

"When are you moving in? I figured we should get started on our dreams right away."

Her heart began a rapid beat inside her chest at the idea. "Didn't I just pack and unpack?"

"And didn't I help you? So, when can we do it again?"

Did she really need to play games? To worry? To wait? When it was right, it was right. "How about we get back to work this week and start packing again this weekend?"

He shook his head. "How about we take the week off—since you'd already planned for that—and move you in right away?"

She met his gaze. The eagerness she saw there matched her own. "Okay," she said softly.

"Good. I love you, Sierra," he said, pressing a kiss against her lips.

"And I love you."

"So when can we go pick out our dog?"

She threw her head back and laughed. This man would not only keep her on her toes but he would make sure he satisfied every dream she'd ever had. And even those she wasn't aware of having.

# Epilogue

*Two years later*

"Jilly, you can't ride the dog!" Sierra called out to her daughter from where she stood in the kitchen baking cookies for the family gathering they were hosting later today. Her brothers, Ryder's brother, and some of their friends were coming.

Named after Ryder's mom, Jillian, their daughter was an adorable mini-me to her mom and a headstrong child, to boot. And right now, she was attempting to climb onto the back of their St. Bernard, Wiley.

The dog was good-natured and only four years old. They'd found him at the shelter when he was approximately two. The original couple who'd had him hadn't anticipated the amount of work and food a dog of his size entailed. And since it would only get worse, Wiley had found his way to the shelter. And into their home.

Sierra had moved in that same week they'd gotten together and started up her home social media company, Knight Time Social, soon after. She'd then gone off birth control and he'd knocked her up immediately, he thought with a grin. She had an assistant she'd hired and the business was growing. He was so damned proud of her.

He walked up behind her and wrapped his arms around her waist, resting his chin on her shoulder. "Hey, sweetheart."

"Hey." She turned in his arms. "Are you here to steal cookie dough?"

"Nope. I'm here to steal a kiss," he said and brushed his mouth over hers, once, twice, before diving in for a real one. He slid his tongue past her lips and devoured her mouth, tasting a hint of chocolate, making him realize she'd been sneaking cookie dough herself.

"How are you?" she asked after he'd broken the kiss, only to come up for air.

"Good. You?" Because their family would be here soon.

"Good. Pregnant."

"Good. I'll make sure we have extra chairs in the family room for— Wait, what?" he asked, her unexpected words sinking in.

"I'm pregnant. Again," she said, her eyes lit up with happiness. "Your sperm are potent, Ryder Hammond. This time you bypassed my birth control."

He was stunned. Yeah, they wanted more kids, but no, they hadn't planned for another one so soon. Not that he was complaining, he thought.

With a whoop, he picked her up and spun her around, placing her down at the same time he felt a tug on his pants.

"Daddy, up!"

Grinning at Sierra, he bent down to pick up their daughter into his arms, then spun her the same way he'd done to her mother.

She giggled, the sound going straight to his heart. "Hey, baby. You're going to be a big sister!"

"Yay!" She clapped her hands happily.

He had no idea if she even understood what he meant. Snaking out an arm, he pulled Sierra in with them, causing Wiley to give a woof, obviously annoyed at being left out.

"Are we telling the family?" he asked.

"I say we keep it to ourselves for another month or two. Unless little mouth here slips up." She kissed Jilly on the nose and she swiped at the spot with her hand.

Ryder's heart swelled with happiness. There was a time he hadn't thought he'd have this—the family, the kids, the dog, the wife, and the bigger house.

"We're going to have to talk about expanding." He'd had plans drawn up for the future, but apparently that time was now.

"Okay."

"Okay." He kissed her and put his wriggling daughter down so she could run after Wiley.

He looked around, his heart full. He woke up every day grateful and glad he'd stood up and objected at Sierra's wedding, taking off with the bride.

Nobody said he wasn't determined when he went about achieving his dreams.

\* \* \* \*

Also from 1001 Dark Nights and Carly Phillips, discover His to Protect.

Sign up for the 1001 Dark Nights Newsletter
and be entered to win a Tiffany Key necklace.

There's a contest every month!

Go to www.1001DarkNights.com to subscribe.

As a bonus, all subscribers can download
FIVE FREE exclusive books!

# Discover 1001 Dark Nights Collection Six

*Go to www.1001DarkNights.com for more information.*

DRAGON CLAIMED by Donna Grant
A Dark Kings Novella

ASHES TO INK by Carrie Ann Ryan
A Montgomery Ink: Colorado Springs Novella

ENSNARED by Elisabeth Naughton
An Eternal Guardians Novella

EVERMORE by Corinne Michaels
A Salvation Series Novella

VENGEANCE by Rebecca Zanetti
A Dark Protectors/Rebels Novella

ELI'S TRIUMPH by Joanna Wylde
A Reapers MC Novella

CIPHER by Larissa Ione
A Demonica Underworld Novella

RESCUING MACIE by Susan Stoker
A Delta Force Heroes Novella

ENCHANTED by Lexi Blake
A Masters and Mercenaries Novella

TAKE THE BRIDE by Carly Phillips
A Knight Brothers Novella

INDULGE ME by J. Kenner
A Stark Ever After Novella

THE KING by Jennifer L. Armentrout
A Wicked Novella

QUIET MAN by Kristen Ashley
A Dream Man Novella

ABANDON by Rachel Van Dyken
A Seaside Pictures Novella

THE OPEN DOOR by Laurelin Paige
A Found Duet Novella

CLOSER by Kylie Scott
A Stage Dive Novella

SOMETHING JUST LIKE THIS by Jennifer Probst
A Stay Novella

BLOOD NIGHT by Heather Graham
A Krewe of Hunters Novella

TWIST OF FATE by Jill Shalvis
A Heartbreaker Bay Novella

MORE THAN PLEASURE YOU by Shayla Black
A More Than Words Novella

WONDER WITH ME by Kristen Proby
A With Me In Seattle Novella

THE DARKEST ASSASSIN by Gena Showalter
A Lords of the Underworld Novella

Also from 1001 Dark Nights:
DAMIEN by J. Kenner

# Discover 1001 Dark Nights

*Go to www.1001DarkNights.com for more information.*

## COLLECTION ONE

## COLLECTION TWO

KISS THE FLAME by Christopher Rice
DARING HER LOVE by Melissa Foster
TEASED by Rebecca Zanetti
THE PROMISE OF SURRENDER by Liliana Hart

**COLLECTION THREE**
HIDDEN INK by Carrie Ann Ryan
BLOOD ON THE BAYOU by Heather Graham
SEARCHING FOR MINE by Jennifer Probst
DANCE OF DESIRE by Christopher Rice
ROUGH RHYTHM by Tessa Bailey
DEVOTED by Lexi Blake
Z by Larissa Ione
FALLING UNDER YOU by Laurelin Paige
EASY FOR KEEPS by Kristen Proby
UNCHAINED by Elisabeth Naughton
HARD TO SERVE by Laura Kaye
DRAGON FEVER by Donna Grant
KAYDEN/SIMON by Alexandra Ivy/Laura Wright
STRUNG UP by Lorelei James
MIDNIGHT UNTAMED by Lara Adrian
TRICKED by Rebecca Zanetti
DIRTY WICKED by Shayla Black
THE ONLY ONE by Lauren Blakely
SWEET SURRENDER by Liliana Hart

**COLLECTION FOUR**
ROCK CHICK REAWAKENING by Kristen Ashley
ADORING INK by Carrie Ann Ryan
SWEET RIVALRY by K. Bromberg
SHADE'S LADY by Joanna Wylde
RAZR by Larissa Ione
ARRANGED by Lexi Blake
TANGLED by Rebecca Zanetti
HOLD ME by J. Kenner

SOMEHOW, SOME WAY by Jennifer Probst
TOO CLOSE TO CALL by Tessa Bailey
HUNTED by Elisabeth Naughton
EYES ON YOU by Laura Kaye
BLADE by Alexandra Ivy/Laura Wright
DRAGON BURN by Donna Grant
TRIPPED OUT by Lorelei James
STUD FINDER by Lauren Blakely
MIDNIGHT UNLEASHED by Lara Adrian
HALLOW BE THE HAUNT by Heather Graham
DIRTY FILTHY FIX by Laurelin Paige
THE BED MATE by Kendall Ryan
NIGHT GAMES by CD Reiss
NO RESERVATIONS by Kristen Proby
DAWN OF SURRENDER by Liliana Hart

**COLLECTION FIVE**
BLAZE ERUPTING by Rebecca Zanetti
ROUGH RIDE by Kristen Ashley
HAWKYN by Larissa Ione
RIDE DIRTY by Laura Kaye
ROME'S CHANCE by Joanna Wylde
THE MARRIAGE ARRANGEMENT by Jennifer Probst
SURRENDER by Elisabeth Naughton
INKED NIGHTS by Carrie Ann Ryan
ENVY by Rachel Van Dyken
PROTECTED by Lexi Blake
THE PRINCE by Jennifer L. Armentrout
PLEASE ME by J. Kenner
WOUND TIGHT by Lorelei James
STRONG by Kylie Scott
DRAGON NIGHT by Donna Grant
TEMPTING BROOKE by Kristen Proby
HAUNTED BE THE HOLIDAYS by Heather Graham
CONTROL by K. Bromberg

HUNKY HEARTBREAKER by Kendall Ryan
THE DARKEST CAPTIVE by Gena Showalter

Also from 1001 Dark Nights:

TAME ME by J. Kenner
THE SURRENDER GATE By Christopher Rice
SERVICING THE TARGET By Cherise Sinclair
TEMPT ME by J. Kenner

# About Carly Phillips

Carly Phillips gives her readers Alphalicious heroes to swoon for and romance to set your heart on fire, and she loves everything about writing romance. She married her college sweetheart and lives in Purchase, NY along with her three crazy dogs: two wheaten terriers and a mutant Havanese, who are featured on her Facebook and Instagram. She has raised two incredible daughters who put up with having a mom as a romance author. Carly is the author of over fifty romances, and is a NY Times, Wall Street Journal, and USA Today Bestseller. She loves social media and interacting with her readers. Want to keep up with Carly? Sign up for her newsletter and receive TWO FREE books at www.carlyphillips.com.

# Discover More Carly Phillips

His to Protect: A Bodyguard Bad Boys/Masters and Mercenaries Novella
by Carly Phillips

Talia Shaw has spent her adult life working as a scientist for a big pharmaceutical company. She's focused on saving lives, not living life. When her lab is broken into and it's clear someone is after the top secret formula she's working on, she turns to the one man she can trust. The same irresistible man she turned away years earlier because she was too young and naive to believe a sexy guy like Shane Landon could want *her.*

Shane Landon's bodyguard work for McKay-Taggart is the one thing that brings him satisfaction in his life. Relationships come in second to the job. Always. Then little brainiac Talia Shaw shows up in his backyard, frightened and on the run, and his world is turned upside down. And not just because she's found him naked in his outdoor shower, either.

With Talia's life in danger, Shane has to get her out of town and to her eccentric, hermit mentor who has the final piece of the formula she's been working on, while keeping her safe from the men who are after her. Guarding Talia's body certainly isn't any hardship, but he never expects to fall hard and fast for his best friend's little sister and the only woman who's ever really gotten under his skin.

# Take Me Down
## Knight Brothers Book 3
## By Carly Phillips

*Next from Carly Phillips in the Knight Brothers series:*

Opposites not only attract, they combust!

Parker Knight was going through the motions… and then he met her.

In sweet, sexy Emily Stevens and the rundown resort she runs with her father, Parker sees the chance to reclaim the life he once lost and take care of the first woman who makes him feel … everything. He wants her in a way he's never desired a woman before and yearns to sample the treats the sexy baker has to offer.

But Emily doesn't trust charming city guys, especially one who is going to leave when his time off is over. No matter how good he makes her feel, in bed or out.

Parker has his hands full, not only with a wary Emily but with someone who doesn't want the lodge to succeed, and if things keep getting worse, not even a Knight can save her.

## On behalf of 1001 Dark Nights,
Liz Berry and M.J. Rose would like to thank ~

Steve Berry
Doug Scofield
Kim Guidroz
Jillian Stein
InkSlinger PR
Dan Slater
Asha Hossain
Chris Graham
Fedora Chen
Kasi Alexander
Jessica Johns
Dylan Stockton
Richard Blake
and Simon Lipskar

Made in the USA
Middletown, DE
23 May 2019